KISSING
COUSINS

Books by Hortense Calisher

NOVELS
False Entry
Textures of Life
Journal from Ellipsia
The New Yorkers
Queenie
Standard Dreaming
Eagle Eye
On Keeping Women
Mysteries of Motion
The Bobby-Soxer
Age

NOVELLAS AND SHORT STORIES
In the Absence of Angels
Tale for the Mirror
Extreme Magic
The Railway Police and the Last Trolley Ride
The Collected Stories of Hortense Calisher
Saratoga, Hot

AUTOBIOGRAPHY
Herself

KISSING COUSINS

A *Memory*

By
Hortense Calisher

WN

Weidenfeld & Nicolson
New York

Copyright © 1988 by Hortense Calisher

Published by Weidenfeld & Nicolson, New York
A Division of Wheatland Corporation
841 Broadway
New York, New York 10003-4793

Published in Canada by General Publishing Company, Ltd.

Library of Congress Cataloging-in-Publication Data

Calisher, Hortense.
Kissing cousins : a memory / by Hortense Calisher. — 1st ed.
p.   cm.
ISBN 1-555-84194-5
1. Calisher, Hortense—Biography—Family.   2. Novelists,
American—20th century—Biography.   3. Jews—Southern States—Social
life and customs.   I. Title.
PS3553.A4Z463   1988
813.′54—dc 19
[B]   88-15729
                                                                        CIP

Manufactured in the United States of America
Designed by Helen Barrow
First Edition
10   9   8   7   6   5   4   3   2   1

KISSING
COUSINS

"Northerners don't chuckle," I said to my kissing cousin, Katie Pyle, although at the moment there wasn't anybody in my parents' living room who had been born in the North, except me.

At fifteen, I considered myself to be having a wretched time in a hard-line New York City school whose teachers never laughed, even at us girls. Here at home, everybody in the room was magnetic enough, but so closely related to me that they were half-obligated to misunderstand me. Due to my father's age, almost all of them were two generations away from me as well, instead of one, and I was their only young.

A kissing cousin, part of the family in every respect except blood, could be more tolerant of flaws to which she wasn't kin, and Katie besides was only twice my age.

Fifteen years older only. Slim in her uniform as a visiting nurse attached to the Henry Street Settlement, Katie had dark circles under her great blue eyes, after a day's work of whose trials she never spoke. Since she had gone against her family's wishes in order to nurse, our own family, a clan of Southern emigrés with similar prides and reticences, never spoke of her vocation either, except to remark among themselves that she was too frail for it, and to welcome her extra warmly when she dropped in.

We were a household of droppers-in, related or not.

"A nation of them," my mother said. Although as a non-Southerner she naturally objected more to those on my father's side. Yet her own relatives, German emigrés and 1880 arrivals to my paternal side's 1820s, were not necessarily in her favor.

"Well—you're all welcome to it," she sometimes said to the kitchen wall over the cook's shoulder, as she supervised the comestibles flowing into the dining room. "All this fracas and hullabaloo."

This was what she had got by marrying into a pack of Southern Jews, who had thereby a double expressiveness, of which one could never be sure which end was up, Jehovah or Jefferson Davis, the president of the Confederacy. Sometimes they hollered so that until you entered a room you might think it was murder. Or else the many sly spinsters among them were so lah-de-dah over the sherry that you half believed their hair combs were tiaras that had slipped—until they gossiped, when they sputtered like knucklebones frying. "How can they?" she said to the wall, which was used to being so addressed. "How can refined people, who have been here for over a hundred years, still be so *loud?*"

Yet, as a latecomer greenhorn emigré of the early 1900s, dumped penniless on a kindly aunt and uncle in York-ville—solid sugar-eating burghers whose wives sat in satin and lace for pictures by Sarony and cooked food no different from their Christian neighbors—my mother now suspected she had done better for herself than they could have, even if she had married a charmer too old for her—who she was no longer so sure was the wrong kind of American.

"Why do Germans always enter a room single file?" she would hiss between her teeth as her side of the family tittupped in on the balls of their feet of a ritual Sunday, for except for my great-aunt, who might come by of a weekday for afternoon coffee, they never dropped in—and even then Tante always brought a cake.

"Simple," my father said. "They have to weigh every word twice."

From our corner that night, Katie and I watched the crowd, all Southerners, since it wasn't Sunday and not a day for the Kaffee-Klatsch. By evening there were always at least three or four extra in our apartment, some of whom would stay to dinner—and there were always corners to watch them from. Aunts and uncles always, as sons and daughters of my father's resident mother, their "Maw." And cousins of every age except mine, up to and beyond my father's, who, pushing seventy, was still his mother's youn-

gest boy. Some relatives had already come and gone during
the day; others would arrive after the evening meal.
Grandma, who never appeared at table but held court in
her own rooms, was of course the reason everybody felt free
to come.

It might be noted that Katie had not answered me imme-
diately. In our house people often didn't, sometimes pick-
ing up on a remark even days afterward. You were expected
to know what was being referred to, and usually did. If not,
a hugely refreshing colloquium might ensue, between
you, the original poser of the remark, and any family
bystander, after which, everything pertinent and a good
deal else having been picked over, we could all return to
base.

My image of our house was that it reverberated with
sounds that had to be classified, and that this was society.
Anything visual about people could come later—and was
a coarse kind of fun. But if you listened well enough, in the
end you heard everything, remembered most of it, and in
the pauses you could think truth.

"No, they cain't, kin they?" Katie said suddenly. "Never
could."

I heard at once how she had changed my statement. I'd
said they didn't; she'd said they couldn't: chuckle. A whole
history might lie between—and were "they" aware of their
incapacity? Meanwhile, I "saw" Katie's words, spelled out.
In our house one had constantly to write dialect in one's
head. Katie and her sister, Rachel, had been born in
Richmond, Virginia, like my father's generation and that of

her father, Solomon Pyle, but, brought North early, had spent their later girlhood in Port Washington, Long Island. Always spoken of among the Pyles as "Port," in my mind it was an estate they had appropriated, which utterly belonged to them and was pronounced Po-ut, much the way some Northerners said "poet"—although in Oral English class at my school our lah-de-dah Miss Cramer encouraged us to make rabbit lips and say "poytry." Port had clarified Katie's accent a little, smoothing out the diphthongs and lessening the lovely, liquid Southern "l," so that while my grown-up cousin Lee, visiting from Richmond, greeted me with a gentle "*Hay*l-lo, Cudd'n Ho-*tay*-uns" all in one gentle coo, Katie said "Hot-tense" and put only one "l" in "del-li-cate." Henry Street duties had quickened her, but would never make her brusque.

Sitting next to me in one of the straight chairs she preferred because of a neck injury suffered when she had served as a nurse with the Allied forces in France, Katie was smiling at the planetary arrangements in our living room. I had begun to think of our small family universe in that way ever since taking Physics at school, a subject that seemed to me as interestingly random and tatty as my family's furniture—particularly the chairs. Whereas other families had suites they had bought in one swoop, our chairs, pursuing us from many prior residences and ancestors, had then jelled on us here. Just so, Physics seemed to be made up of subjects that had no other place to go at the moment, and even our teachers seemed uncertain when they taught it, as if they had just then studied it up—which was quite probable, since not one of those manic devotees of education had chosen it as her specialty.

I myself knew too well what I felt about Math—an awesome alpine range into whose purity I could never climb. English was meanwhile a kind of woodshed, where I could rummage for words and even turn up other necessaries—like in the back rooms of those odd dealerships that sold both coal and ice.

But Physics was more like our own household, full of closets that scarcely knew any longer what they held, in whose depths I could spend an afternoon with the concrete. One minute you were only learning at what temperature water would boil, like in any kitchen. Then suddenly you were seeing what iron filings did—whang— when you inched a horseshoe magnet too near on their bit of white blotting paper. Then—swoosh—out to astronomy's heavens, to check on what Miss Yeager, the perennial substitute who got stuck with all the odds and ends, nervously wielding her colored chalks at the blackboard, had called "our planetary family, girls. Man the telescopes!"

Here I was with my telescope at home. Over in one corner my father's sisters were squabbling in accordance with their time-tried pecking order. Two sisters-in-law, widows of my father's brothers, held another corner, in clear abstention from them. Soon my father's sister Aunt Flora would grab him—now visiting his mother down the hall—to suggest a poker game. He had a poker night "outside" once in a while but never liked to have a game in the house, because Flora would join it, whipping toward the table like an iron filing—and Flora crowed when she won.

Once, I had been sent with cigars down a few blocks to the Walter Markens' house, where my father did play, and had glimpsed that silent male House of Poker Parliament under the hanging lamp of Markens' dining table. We had a lamp just like it, but it bred only vast dinners, or dress patterns to be cut—for me, until the time when I would gravitate to that dressmaker who, like the cigarmaker, the butcher, and the house superintendent, was one of the satellites who helped our family crew retain its place.

In our dining room at the moment my Uncle Clarence, Flora's husband, was laying out solitaire, while Harry B., my father's bookkeeper and courtesy brother-in-law (as brother to one of the widowed sisters-in-law), siphoned his marital troubles into Clarence's left ear. Harry had cheated my father once but had been taken back into the fold after discovery, his only apparent punishment being that he had lost his name to an initial, and must forever float our cosmos as Harry B.

Uncle Clarence, a sweet man with the large, noble features that seemed to me to be somehow linked with the enormous tolerance of the henpecked—and not too much later with stomach cancer—revolved alone, except for the Sunday walks he took me on when my father was away on business. A couple of the older spinster second cousins from Newark, New Jersey—to me an unknown hutch of a place that sprouted only their ilk and was accessible only by a Tube—fussed around my mother, who never sewed in the evening but had brought out some handiwork to show. One of my father's five nieces hung by her.

Jessica, a teacher, was a regular here—as she would be to the end of her life. My other first cousins—Amy, Gertrude, Ann, and Grace, all grown women also, out on the fringes studying opera and other glamor pursuits or about to marry men in Wall Street—rarely came.

The two handsomest, Amy and Gertrude, were said to be forbidden here altogether, because their mother, my pretty, white-haired Aunt Belle, widow of my Uncle Nat, though a Jew herself was trying to pass them off as Christians—and they were acceding. I liked Belle for the airy, marquise style with which she already treated me, as the woman I would someday maybe be. I thought I understood her foibles and suspected my father did also, and might even have tolerated these, in a foolish woman who was after all only a sister-in-law and not geared to the austerity that underlay all our rococo appearances, as well as a sister to such as Harry B. But her daughters, my own blood, I could not forgive, approving utterly of my father's rumored ukase against them, even though I suspected they couldn't care less and might even be relieved at the excuse to sever ties.

Their own dead father's Certificate of Merit from the Public Schools of Richmond: "Awarded to Nathan Calisher, a pupil in 34d Primary Central School No. 34, for correct DEPORTMENT and diligent attention to STUDIES for four successive weeks—Session 1875–

76"—attested to by a Miss L. M. Hicks in the brown
tracery common to so much old document—was in our
big leatherbound family Bible, along with, it is only fair to
say, a pressed maple leaf that made me sad and a receipt,
issued to my grandfather for insurance on a slave, that
made me queasy, since according to my father our grandmother had never kept any servants except the freed. Perhaps my grandfather, of whom I knew only the severe space
between nose and mouth in his mutton-chopped portrait,
had been of another mind.

In any case it was all our heritage, and those girls were
burning it behind them. As a boy my Uncle Nat, like my
father, must surely have had to attend afternoon Hebrew
School, when released by Miss Hicks. He survived, to die
as an elder when I was about seven, of what I had always
thought to be a young person's disease—TB. In a large
cabinet photograph taken not too long before, he looks
appropriately bewildered. We had all long since become
only moderately religious to the outward eye, mostly Sunday School and confirmation for me and my brother, and
synagogue for my father on the high holy days, plus his
occasional reading from the Hebrew, partly to show us how
it was done and that he still could, but also to mellow
himself in a language whose beauties he wanted made
plain. Even in his generation, intermarriages had been
made—and ingested into the clan. But on his side (on
which I most surely was), none of this had made us feel any
less proudly Jewish. What we had kept was a moral severity—some would call it overweening—akin to that

unyielding vertical between my grandfather's mouth and nose. Inside me I had a similar perpendicular, against which I could measure conduct, mine and other people's, in order to keep us all in line.

It went like this: Jehovah, in whom I no longer believed or perhaps had never quite believed, had nevertheless planted His ethical standard inside me. Since I doubted that He would bother to lean down from on high to pass judgment, say, on those two poor creatures who were ashamed of what He was to them, I would have to do it for Him.

I had no idea that this high-mindedness was an essential of the Jewish style. Or that this, too, had its variations, running a gamut from my father's thundering condemnation of what to him sinned equally against his pride in Jewish history and his pride in himself, to those high-coiffed ladies, now perched by preference on our more fragile love seats, who merely thought it tacky of Cousin Gertrude to have changed her name to Pat. But I already felt the sweet tribal comfort to be got from such action, though I wasn't quite sure of my perch. "Tacky," like "gemütlich," was one of the untranslatables that so much affected the attitudes of our household—and perhaps because of this, words and their possible exactitudes were where I was beginning to put my trust.

I slipped closer to Katie on her chair, even leaning against her, though just short of twining myself on her, as someone of our steady flow of visitors from Virginia might have done. We had many other kissing cousins among

Richmond families as anciently close to us as the Pyles were, but most of them still lived down there, sending us a stream of their famous cupcakes, and when they came up North, forming a sugary oasis in our living room with their fond if shallow ways. Twining was one of these. I yearned after this fondness and saw what it could do for one, but my mother, who had trouble being fond, saw it as "They're always all over you," and forbade me it.

"Gertrude's changed her name to Pat," I said. "Katie, that's tacky, isn't it?" When she didn't answer right off, I said, "Maybe she doesn't know there are German girls named Trudy." I knew lots of girls who didn't like their names just as names, and I was one of them, thinking mine pretentious because it was French and I wasn't—and in English either syllable emphasized sounded wrong. So I wanted to be fair—another cheeseparing burden of the verbal.

Katie knew all this, as well as perhaps why I had chosen her to know—as I did not. But I could hear the synagogue, if not Sunday School in her voice, intentionally soft. "Hon', in Gertrude's case it's mo' than tacky." Then she patted my knee, as two new contingents entered. Martin Freeman, my father's accountant, and the nice lady he lived with (his wife being in the looney bin), who on my father's insistence, counter to the ladies, had finally become persona grata here. After him, a stranger?—no, it was "Uncle" Louis Arnstein, a courtesy uncle from Philadelphia, in whose widower household I and my father had once stayed. Following him was Erna, an oily-skinned

German girl sent us as an emigrant after the war, and maybe even a cousin, but so sweaty lower-class and so groaningly stupid that my mother, refusing to admit cousinship, had made a maid of her, until Erna found a man, again in a way my mother could not approve. Well, here was Erna with him in tow—and on the wrong day.

Yes, we had our orbits, although clearly my mother, now crimping her lips from across the room at Katie, also her favorite, didn't think of them as heavenly. Sometimes, looking out at her domain here of an evening, or in the quiescence at table when the cloth was finally being crumbed, she had a phrase she breathed, ostensibly not for anyone to hear. "And so forth," she would say under her breath. "And . . . so-o forth."

It was not the same as *und so weiter*, I thought, on the translating tape in my head. She was now an American.

Katie winked back at her. She was an intimate of both of us—a neat accomplishment, though she wouldn't have considered it so. As with so many Southern women I saw, cronydom came naturally to her, and age was no barrier. Her allegiance to me had begun when she had wheeled me in my baby carriage, she at the age I was now. "Gone ten minutes and your pah-puh came steaming around the block. Thought I'd lost you, hon'." I hear the cadence: *lost you—hon'*. Affection was never better stated in a pause. As for me, my cleaving to Katie predated memory, and perhaps even that overstuffed carriage, of which a picture of me in it the first time I was allowed out survived, as well as the legend that my father, in order to show off his belated firstborn in her open-air debut, had donned a three-button cutaway and top hat and had paraded me down Fifth Avenue.

Since although his office was there we lived nowhere near that avenue, I had long since taken this story under advisement, for further consideration during one of those pauses for truth. It seemed to me that Southerners, like Jews, had a special talent for telling stories but, unlike Northerners, knew very well when not to believe in them. Northerners of any persuasion seemed to me altogether awash when it came to anecdote. Or to family myth—if they had any, which was doubtful as far as I could tell. They seemed to learn even their jokes logically, in order to save them up for a later day. Had they no ragbag of old faithfuls, such as the genealogical oddities that snaked out onto our dinner table from behind the starched napkins? Or the chronicles of sickness that crept out into the sewing circle while some members stayed overlong in the bathroom? Or, best of all, those whoppers that spewed up, lusty and outrageous, in the hollering. If Northerners, as evinced by my school friends or our New York visitors, did have any free-flowing intimacy like ours, they must keep it dark or, again, save up for it. Anyway, even if they did have planetary systems in their own households, I felt sure that, by contrast, we were the planets who sang.

As for my Jewishness, that was satisfyingly in all of me, no more to be questioned than the body I walked around in. And Katie Pyle was the same only more so, for the three Pyle women—Katie, her mother (my Aunt Beck), and her sister, Rachel (self-styled Nita)—went much to the consolations of the synagogue, why so I wouldn't know fully until Katie was old. But I knew that in the eyes of my mother, who never went there at all, although she could well have used consolations, Katie, already seemingly so removed from the marital by her vocation, was in danger of becoming one of those single women who went too much to God.

Meanwhile, I could see for myself how Katie's Southernness overlay her Jewishness yet united with it, as evinced in her looks. I wouldn't see until years later that her face much resembled Bette Davis's in its lively responses as well as its features, not barring the slightly pulled bit of nose between the nostrils.

It could indeed be a Christian face unless you looked carefully. Its ancestry was Dutch and German, her mother having been a Rebecca Boettigheimer, and its coloring blond. Jews more used to the Sephardic strains and brunette complexion I bore might not recognize her as Jewish at all. But unlike my mother, whose chestnut Teuton beauty could blush with pleasure at a "Why, I wouldn't have known you *were*," Katie never spoke of her own looks in any Jewish-Christian context and, I knew for sure, would have been angered by any such compliment.

Of course I never really saw her more than gently angry until she was eighty. But she was the epitome of what in the days of the Gibson Girl era slightly before her was called "spunk." Indeed, the special link between us came of that quality, and the story of how this happened seemed to me as grisly cute as some of the folklore sent my father each month by a Hebrew subscription society—and equally as Jewish as a tale could be.

One night, when I was a tot, I had a fever, as tots in those less inoculated days seemed more to do, either surviving by their own dower of resistance or not. "Katie, thank God,"—this is my father speaking—"was student-nursing just then, and happened to be there."

Hanging on the tale, which was never to be dribbled at too slow a pace for me, I knew just how that would be. Tired after her exhausting hours of day service, or else facing the prospect of a long hospital night, Katie would have come by to this place that was hers in all but blood, drawn in less by the abundance of food than by the hectic glow of the company, even whose quarreling amused her. Of course she would be fed, and expected to be. But not in the way of other droppers-in, who, as many times as they came, had to be invited and pressed to stay several times over of an evening in a number of variations suited to the circumstances of each, had in fact to be confirmed of their welcome all the harder because frequently they knew damn well they weren't.

"Oh, come, I made a jellied salad," my mother might say too winningly to an aunt who hated it and might well criticize our excellent cuisine—in which such salad was not normal—as tartly as if she had paid for it. Or, "Now, Martha," my father might say carefully to the poorest cousin from Newark. "Take something, before that ride."

And mincingly or haughtily, or even hungrily, their protestations would subside.

Katie never protested, but not only because she was honestly welcome. She took as her right the expansive Southern hospitality she had been reared in—if we were ever to be at her house she and hers would be sure to make return in kind. I saw also how she returned our hospitality in the same moment it was extended, by the grace with which she accepted, honoring the food with a light, sincere aside—"Hattie, this is exceptional"—to my mother, whose awkward bridal efforts were family lore, but whose mature day-to-day efforts, taken for granted now by all, went unpraised. Or I would hear Katie joining in the talk with a modest sliver of a laugh, not too lyrically shaped.

I supposed that France had given her poise—"Gay Paree" being all I knew of it other than a rosy-ruffled bisque doll, presented me when I was thought to be too young for it, that danced on its platform, inclining its pink mobcap, and then disappeared into a cupboard forever in what I assumed was the French style. But when I once dared to ask Katie about her French experience—during and after World War I it would have been, with the wounded—tears started in her eyes and were held there while the eyes widened, a phenomenon I had never seen before; maybe this was Southern, too?

I wouldn't have my answer until I was in graduate school and dined one night in Harlem at a black schoolmate's home table, where I might observe in my schoolmate's

mother the same hospitality, the same soft shoots of laugh-
ter—and when she spoke of her first experience here up
North, as one of the just-arrived girls who in the early
morning had stood in street-corner slave markets in the
Bronx, to be picked off as slavies for the day by the local
Jewish housewives—that same brimming of the eyes.

I was old enough by then to know that it couldn't be
Southern exclusively, to hold back tears in that way, not
letting them drop. Or to save up memory, as with our
household's every closet and chair. Yet I was still young
enough to note what my elders at home, my father, my
courtly uncles and their retinue of women, all of them
cosseting our household help with the usual "We know
how to treat them decently," had never admitted to themselves or maybe never even seen—that in the curious way
the *droit de seigneur* redounds even on the kind master who
will not exercise it, they had learned some of their soft
manners from the Blacks.

"You not too Northern, Girl, seemlike," my friend's
mother said, settling back from emotion into her own
amplitude and regally dishing out. On my first visit she
hadn't called me Girl; now she had grown more daring. I
knew that after rising to the status of full-time maid she had
married an accountant with his own agency on 125th
Street. On one corner of that famous cross street, my father
had once pointed out to me, as we were driven by, a big
gray apartment house shaped like the Flatiron Building
and new when he came to New York, into which he as the
youngest son, who though still in his twenties had done

well in the North, had brought my grandparents and family and all their worldly goods—including the massive bed on which I still slept.

"Wait to hear how she tell a story, Mahma," my schoolmate said. "Slow as molasses in the mawning." She was writing her Master's thesis in the Speech Department at Teacher's College. At home her style of talk reverted, although never all the way.

Katie, addressing her own mother, said "Mahma" in just that deferent, drawn-out way. My Cousin Lee, still living in Richmond and even closer to the heritage, said "Mah Daydee and Mumma," just like their own maid. Though of course their grammar was not affected.

"Oh, do I?" I said too loud. Did the twinge of guilt I felt come from the North—and the ache underlying it from the South? "It's memory that's slow." Why did I feel that they here would understand this better than anybody else—except us?

"You wrap a story plumb round a spool," my friend said. Looking down the table at her silent father and brothers, she hooted, maybe a little too loud also. "Zackly like us."

"Like you and Mother," the elder boy said.

I smiled too hard, because the tape in my head was still running on. Even in fun, we none of us would ever have said "plumb."

"Uh-*huh*—" her mother said, in emphasis. "That the case?"

If, on the other hand, mild denial were intended, she and we would have let loose an "*uh*-uh," in a lowercase, casual voice, modestly inserted. I heard, too, now how at home our affirmatives had always been much stronger than our negatives.

"Ah-hah?" her mother said now. It was as soft as a question could be. "But I'll never believe, uh-*uh*, not on the saddest day, that you is a Jew."

What would Katie have said, in the gentle voice used maybe to patients she had to chide—"Now, y'all!"?

My friend saw my face. "Finish about your cousin," she said in her crispest Teacher's College voice.

"Well, like I said," I said. "She was the cousin visited Shirley when she was a girl."

Shirley was the great plantation along the James River on which my friend's mother had been born—this was why I had been brought here. Mahma would crave to know anybody who even knew what the name Shirley meant down there, my friend had said.

"She was invited there just before they came North," I said. "Some ole Miz Somebody who lived there invited her. That was where she learned to fish, and to ride." And to shoot, though I wasn't sure I should say it. The fishing was unladylike enough. "She stayed three months."

Then her father, "old Solly Pyle" as my father called him, had come to get her. I could see him as I myself had later, a handsome, white-crested man with a fine bearing, dressed in the same summer pongees and Panama hat my father wore—though of course Solomon Pyle would have been younger then. "She says visits were longer in those days. Took a time to get there."

But Pahpa, she'd said, *he was worried I might have fallen for some boy down there.* I heard Katie's laugh, one stave above a chuckle—*Warn't inny me-en at Shirley inny moah. Jus' some ole leftover ladies Mahma'd met in Richmond.* Who were *open to a little young company. Mahma said it would be a precious experience for me. She only let me go because we were already set to move—*

I bet you were the prettiest theng, I'd said stoutly. *You still are.* For I knew my mother and aunts thought now that she would never marry. She'd pursed her lips at them, over there in their corner; she knew that, too. *Not too bad*, she'd said. And was it then it began to sift to me that she must already have had her romance?

"Sure would like to know the name that ole Miz," my friend's mother said. "Course, there was a heap of houses on Shirley. My granddaddy was head inside servant up at the main one."

Down the table her husband cracked a hard roll in his fist and set it on his butter plate. I hadn't seen one of those plates recently; we seldom brought them out even for company. I saw that the two younger boys, who were looking at their father apprehensively, hadn't known to set their butter knives at the edge.

"Tell Mahma how that cousin saved your life as a baby," my friend said. "And only a kissing cousin."

One of the boys snickered. "Kissing cousins. What the f——, heck is that?"

His mother heaved up her bosom, a word I hadn't

thought of since an aunt had noted I was getting one. "It mean close in all but blood. Times I think you not even that to this house, boy." She lifted her chin at her husband, queenly. "Tell your story, Girl."

Southerners tell a story over and over without shame.

So I told how Katie, coming into the nursery, had looked down at the hot child. "You were burning up," my father had said. "I'd already called Kozak." Doctors were known by their last names only in our house, in a kind of ownership.

"I could smell the fever before I saw you," Katie'd said, chiming in. "You must have had over a hundred and five. I knew what it was at once—seen it in the wards. Children don't have it anymore."

"Diphtheria," my father had said. "My heart sank in my shoes." Then he would smile at Katie, saying to the rest of us, "And even then, that girl never raised her voice." It was his specific for women—mostly an unsatisfied one. "And then—" he would say.

But Katie always made an excuse to leave the room at this point, saying, "Hush, hush, Uncle Joe, haow you drahmatize"—after which he would whistle, and fall still. And maybe tell us later, maybe not, depending.

"She always claimed the doctor did it when he came," my father would whisper, looking over his shoulder. "What had to be done, to save you." She was only a student nurse, and she didn't want her parents to know. They might have taken her out of nursing school. She'd had an awful fight to go.

"It forms a false membrane in the throat," I told my friend's table, who were all listening now, even the boys. "You have to suck it out, mouth to mouth. You have to take it in your own throat. And that's what she did."

When I myself put it to her, the first time I heard it, she'd said, "Oh, hush, child. I never catch a thing."

"Sure like to swap talk with that lady from Shirley," my friend's mother said when I was saying good-bye. Their hallway had a comfy, musty smell like ours used to, maybe from the same kind of leather davenport—another word and object I had now left behind me, when after my grandmother's death we had moved to the smaller apartment where my mother was at last free of the clan dinners, and maybe missed the regularity, the grandeur.

"Oh, Mother, her cousin is not *from* Shirley," my friend said. I could have made that correction myself, but knew better. Although I'd never been South I knew that region's grandiosity, white or black, in which in one evening's hearsay a grandfather might slip from being a "boy" somewhere on the "*ess*-state" to being a butler in the mansion house.

"She's a superintendent of nurses now," I said proudly. "But I bet she'd come. She'd be interested to. And I do thank you for that lovely meal. It was like home." Or like home when we went to Flora's, where my father took his hankering for okra, creamed corn off the cob, and oyster dishes Germans had never heard of. I looked around for the father and the boys, but they were gone. "Thank you kindly," I said. It twanged in my ear like a requiem.

"I wanted Arnella to train for a nurse," her mother said. "It stays with you. But col-lege—" She said it with that delicate double "l." Shaking her head at Arnella and me— at what going there had made of us. "Well, come again," she said. "You talk more Southern than my own chile."

Outside on East 110th Street I figured out that Arnella lived at about the same distance from Columbia as I did on Riverside Drive.

"I'll walk you," she said. "Gotta late class."

As we parted on Broadway she said nervously: "Hope you don't mind what she said about Jews. She had a hard time."

I said I didn't—and I didn't.

"I sometimes feel worse about being a Northerner. Or even a Southerner. But in the Jew department? Nothing can touch me there."

Next time Katie dropped in at home I did ask her if she would go. She was regarding our new living room absently. The apartment was decent enough, but there was no grandmother wing, and in the family there had been other decimations. At four o'clock, the former coffee hour, light from the river fell askance on two barrel-shaped chairs that curved forward, empty-armed. The furniture came at us to be noticed now; it had always been subsidiary.

"Good grief, y'all are in reduced circumstances as regards relations, aren't you?" she said. "But the view is nice. Sure, hon'—where did you say?"

When she understood clearly she gave me a long look. Her eyes were still big enough in her face to be called "teacup eyes," as I had once said of them when small, the aunts shrilling behind me, "Saucer eyes, the child means. You mean saucer!" I arguing—"No! Teacup!"—and they teasing on until I cried, and Katie, squeezing her eyes shut to settle the matter, had taken me on her lap to be consoled.

"Hon', you sure do get into things," she said now. Then she chuckled. "Sure I'll go. Sure." Then we hugged.

"Whoosh, I'm tired," she said then. Her face had always been wan, with an even delicacy that as she aged I came to know as the ultimate health, but by now her mouth drooped some at the sides. "Been doing some night duty in the mental ward."

She had never wholly given up nursing, and this was her specialty, her interest dating, she had not long before told me, from the time my own mother, released from a sanatorium after a breakdown following my brother's birth, had been ordered by the doctors to "rest cure" at Atlantic City, with seven-year-old me along to cheer her, and Katie to oversee. "We were there for three months," she'd said at the time, "—don't you recall?"

What I recalled was that I hadn't cheered. My mother, exhorted to the beach, stood fixedly at the hotel window, I behind her, at her waist but ignored. "Come away from that window, child," I'd heard Katie's voice back then say—had she said the final *d* on "child" or not? Even at seven I'd known that her anxiety about the high window was for my mother, not for me. "No," I'd said carefully, when reminded of that time, "I only remember the pony rides."

Now Katie said musingly, "Shirley. How you hold on to things. Forgot I told you 'bout that."

I heard how she got more Southern when she talked of the South, just as my own accent came back on me when I talked to anybody from down there. "I could tell you about your whole visit. Except"—I hesitated—"what did you shoot?"

"Rabbit," she said dreamily. "And once a woodchuck the field hands cooked and I had a taste of. Ugh. Was it fat! 'Supposed to taste like shoat,' I told Mahma when I got home, 'but it don't,' and Mahma laughed 'til she crah'ed. 'Don't ever tell your poppa you ever tasted shoat,' she said. 'Alright to tell him you shot one, though, 'case you did.' And then she laughed some mo'.".

Katie had rosied, the way she always did with stories, and looked younger, as always when she spoke of her adored mother. She drank deep of the coffee I had brought her.

"What's a shoat?"

Civil War Richmond, when my father was born, had been not too many steps above a country town. He had left it early and, so far as I knew, had never shot anything; his sports as a young man were going to cockfights and to boxing matches in the days of brass knuckles, and, until he had married my mother when in his fifties—women.

"Pigling." Katie's mouth quirked. "Tastes right good, way the dawkies at Shirley cooked it." She had spent nearly as much time with them, she'd once said, as she had with the ladies.

At home we had observed no dietary laws. Until I was grown I hadn't even known that the shellfish we consumed in such quantities was forbidden the orthodox—until an acquaintance happened to allude to it. Yet my father, who had eaten everything in his time, professed to disdain pork more as lower class than as a religious sin, and we had never had it.

Now she sighed—the remembering sigh that purled like an undercurrent from all the elders in my father's family, and that I sometimes thought of as the voice of the deserted South speaking through them. Katie, I thought, had learned it too young.

"Those black people were practically keeping the place together for the old ladies. Better nigras I've never seen."

I held very still. I found myself holding my breath. In the new living room there was now a big transformer attached to our radio–record-player, to convert our electricity from direct current to alternating. The apartment house, owned by Columbia University, was among the last in the city still to have DC. I felt like that transformer, my two currents interchanging.

"Arnella—she has a degree." My voice cracked. "She talks like you and me. I mean—like N'Yawk." I heard the tape. When I was with Arnella I talked like she did: I said Noo Yaw-uk.

I felt myself turn red. I did this so seldom that when it happened the whole family rushed to see.

Katie stopped dead. Like a brook stopping. This was another thing I learned—at that instant. Real Southerners ran on, yes, like a brook, detouring round a bad moment like water round a pebble, filling in the chinks of confrontation with a babble, murmuring to a pause. Hollering was a different thing entirely; it was like healthful exercise. It was only Northerners who stopped dead, ominously, like teachers, or like the couples one sometimes saw on the tough streets around grade schools, squaring off like cats and dogs before a fight, the women arching their backs, the men splatting their feet.

Not Katie. When she came to a stop she seemed merely to grow more like herself, on what you might call an "on hold" basis, those eyes dilating at me the way a movie brings you a close-up.

"Whah—yew," she said, in that chiding, half-amused drawl Southern mothers use to remonstrate with a child. "Whah *yew!*" Then her face came back to still. I could see what a student nurse might suddenly find there if a procedure went wrong. My easy father, who hated scolding anybody, would take to quoting Robbie Burns: "Something gone agley, darlin'?"—leaving you uncertain of anything except his love. But Katie meant business.

"Now you hearken, my little cousin," she said. "I *trained* up here with my black sisters. Nights on double duty I slept in the same bey-ud. My schoolmate Marnine Tooker writes me from Atlanta every year. My head cawdiac nurse right now, I would trust her with my life. And she me."

I did hearken. I heard the "my."

She cupped my face in her hands. Just so she had done

when we and my mother had had to leave Atlantic City sooner than planned. *Your mother has to go inside for a while again, dawlin'. And your daddy still has to be away awhile, on business. You're coming down to us, at Port.*

Now she chuckled, not releasing me. "Why you dirty li'l ole No'therner. At Shirley—what the dickens were you thinking I went out to shoot?"

But Katie and I never did visit Arnella's, though we had had the invitation, a large greeting card with red, blue, and gold flowerets, in the middle of which a good round hand, surely her mother's, had inscribed the date and the hour, Six O'clock Supper, and both our names. Four days before, I got a note through Student Mail to meet Arnella at Friedgen's, the Teacher's College haunt. Over their famous brownies she said, "Have to take back that invite. I'm sorry. My parents had a big fight over it. Shall I level with you why?"

What a girl Arnella was, a leveler shooting straight for the whites of one's eyes. And if I may say with the immodest pride we take in our youth once we are mortally separate from it, what a girl was I, humbly brooding on what I was with all the arrogance of the beginner who believes in change.

Sometimes I think of memory as a Sistine Chapel.

Down there on the sunny floor are all the early figures of
life's morning, still as busy as ever they were at that time; up
here on the ceiling are the swollen, over-muscled shapes
we have become; ceiling and floor are powerless to meet.
Which is the ultimate viewer? Which the most alive?

Anyway, good prospects as we two were—for what? The
world's grace?—we muffed it.

"You don't have to," I said. "It's because I'm Jewish.
Your mother had second thoughts. It doesn't matter."

I was too cool about that, I've thought since. Maybe I
should have made like it did matter. The worst of race
relations is for either side to be impervious.

"No, it was my father," Arnella said. I would have said
her voice was too high-tone, if I hadn't known from home
how hysteria closets itself in the too polite. "My father
married down, or thought he did. My mother, as you saw,
is not educated. But she's light. He's dark. And what it
comes to is—" She made a face. "Neither'n can get the
best of t'other. So—he hates Shirley. It's what made her
light-skinned. So he's laid down the law to her. In our
house, which is his house, she can't have anybody white."

The brownies were double chocolate, the darkest ever. I
chewed down the rest of mine. My European mother
laughed at such sweets—gingerbread, angel food cake,
any of that American stuff—the way she did at men drink-
ing malteds, as Columbia College students were doing at
other tables right here. Compared to our confections at
home, fragrant with hazelnut, orange water and kirsch,

and deeper liqueurs, and a subtler bitter chocolate, the brownie did seem to me simpleminded, naive. A Christian cake.

"Oh, Arnella." I leaned forward, loose-breasted in my dance class leotard, scattering the crumbs on my plate. Under her schoolgirl's collar she was flat-chested, and, though older, somehow more callow than me. Yet she had an intensity, stiff as it was, that I might never catch up with. "Oh, Arnella—you're divided. Just like me."

I invited her home to see for herself. And maybe to test my own family's rectitude. After all, we now had German maids only. My father, who still said "colored" when referring to domestics but "nee-gro" otherwise, would simply stand fast on his good manners, on which I knew I could depend. My mother, who had called each of our former maids *die Schwarze,* as if they had no separate being, would be wroth at me for my foolish social ardors, but only behind the scenes.

But Arnella never came. She had more sense.

And though Katie, like many Southerners, belonged to such a visiting family, she never further inquired of me why we didn't get to go.

I remember nothing of that first emergency visit to Port.

On my second visit, three years later when I was ten, of which I remember everything, Nita, Katie's slightly younger sister, who in the family gossip was "some pretty" but too plump to keep it going, and rather sly, said: "When Katie brought you here from Atlantic City, you were such a solemn little thing. Wanted to tell us right off why you were here."

"Rachel—" my Aunt Beck said. She never called her younger daughter by anything but her first given name. I heard the warning, and remembered it, but like so much in that seemingly bland and to me delightful household, the explanation of Nita's sidelong remark, as well as a final account of much else, wasn't to be given to me until a generation later, when I would visit Katie in her eighty-third year, she by then long since retired to a second Port—Port Charlotte, Florida—and we two survivors of households would sort it all out. "Whatever did I say, the first time I came, that Nita wanted to tell?" Nita was dead by then and I would cede her any name she wanted. "I nagged you to tell me, but you always sheared off"—and Katie had laughed, saying, "We were expert at that in the old days, weren't we."

Then her face had solemned, just as it had when I had attended the Florida synagogue with her the day before. "You know, hon', your mother was suicidal? She had taken something once, at home. Doctors said she had to be away from home, from that whole household. Pore Uncle Joe—your father—he never could understand why. That was part of the trouble. But of course he adored her. So I was deeded to take her down there. And then, when I was about to bring her back, looked like she was about to try again. I don't know how you knew. Nothing was on the surface. But when you entered our door at Port you looked up at Aunt Beck with that li'l old face of yours and said: 'We had to leave that hotel. Its windows were too wide.' "

The Port of those days, a small, high white house with porch steps to be sat on, was probably quite close to its next-door neighbors, but with all the bushy Long Island summer to expand in, and the "shore" close by. Deep within, and pervading all just as if Aunt Beck had not had to leave her massive wedding furniture behind her, was the very core and day-to-day persistence of a not quite small-town or small-time Southern and Jewish household in the capital city of Richmond, Virginia, circa 1891—the date inside Beck's broad wedding band deeded to me by Katie, which I sometimes now wear.

Such houses are tenacious, era to era. A palace destroyed can be hard to resurrect—too cumbersome, or perhaps too original. But take a kitchen full of modest husbandry—curds draining in their cheesecloth sock, biscuit-cutter and beach plum jelly waiting on the counter-side—then add a darkish hall where the china closet resides with its hoard of gilt-on-white wedding service or early blue willow ware, go past the dining and living rooms, each with a mood and a time-set like a pub's, then up to the bedroom cubicles with their counterpanes, there perhaps to flop belly down and muse almost atop a tree, while the screen door skreeks, in the cellar the mousetraps snap, and all through the house conversation ripples its common rill—and you could be anywhere, anytime, in one of the forty-eight states of the past.

Aunt Beck always dressed as if she knew this. Her short-sleeved, faintly patterned or white garment, neither a housedress nor quite a tailored shirtdress, was neutral enough for anywhere, either in town or in her own house, as well as at the shore. I hadn't yet seen her counterparts in Back Bay, Boston, or old California in places where the movies hadn't taken over, or even New York's supposedly long-gone Murray Hill—though I would have recognized them. But once, in the big central outdoor plaza of a childhood haunt of mine, the Museum of the American Indian up at 155th Street and Broadway, there had been an exhibition devoted to statues of the American pioneer woman, big white marble effigies with whose bearing I felt quite at home. They all had Beck's same squared-off stance, firm jaw, and air of fortitude. Obviously marble couldn't twinkle with humor or pick up its skirts to wade after mussels. Otherwise, except for a couple of winged and helmeted sculptures who couldn't possibly have been addressed as Awnt, I would have been pleased to visit any one of them in her mythical house.

There the husbands, big and impressively mannered like Solly Pyle, and with the same large geniality even to persons of my age, would have been as infrequently at home as he. So was my father often away on business, but he had an actual office and factory to be away from, and brothers at the corners of each, to weigh them down. Solly Pyle's affairs appeared to float; he was "in jewelry at one time"; was he what my father and his friends called—at the very best—a "representative"? From their confabs I knew quite accurately what each of these men dealt in, but I never knew the nature of Solly's "merchandising," as they would have called it. Whatever he did deal in, I had the impression it was "from time to time," a phrase that in our house did not indicate durability. To our urban clan neither did choosing "the country" to live in all year round. My mother, for sure, had once hinted that Pyle was "a big blow," but then she wasn't trustworthy on the subject of a Southern male expansiveness that perhaps no longer charmed her (as it still magicked me) now that she lived with it. Anyway, unlike his daughter Katie, Solomon Pyle, whose family had been as close as close to ours in Richmond, was never an intimate of our house. I must have seen him there, though, in a long-ago summer, for I remember the hat, the pongee suit, and the flirt of his cane.

In Port that second visit of mine, it was summer, too, and he was in once or twice—and out again. Although dressed less grandee, he was as courtly as I'd thought he would be, oddly so even to his children, and to his wife, who addressed him frontally as "Solly Pyle," calling him that in his absence as well. Whenever home he was treated as absolute god, because to Beck that was what husbands were. He was never heavy about it but seemed to expect that treatment and enjoy it, if briefly. I was already used to men who gave the appearance of taking the most excellent wifely cuisine and solicitude as homely cures for more sophisticated routines outside, but though I tried I could never imagine what his routines were, and somehow never called him Uncle, as I had been trained to address all other male familiars of his age. Whenever he left us at Port, always saying that he'd be "looking in again shortly"—just as at home the Fuller Brush Man did—his son Aaron ("Ayron"), addressed by his sisters as "Brother," became substitute god.

From Brother I learned more about women in such a household than I wanted to. I had been lucky, as the first and cherished child of a man past middle age, who saw no reason why she should not be "brainy" as well, perhaps because his own mother, daughter of a rabbi and sister of a philosopher, had been the same. When a son and heir finally arrived, I was "Sister" for a while, but in that half-breed household this soon fizzled out.

The sisters Pyle were sisters to the nth. Clearly, at the synagogue they were first of all audience and working "Sisterhood"—the actual name of the Jewish women's auxiliary, to which even at ten I privately vowed I would never belong because of what that did to you. Elsewhere at the synagogue, the Pyle women were always faithfully attendant in every category where they were allowed to fit in; they kept the vestal light. Aaron somehow functioned there whether he attended services regularly or not—exactly like the Lord Adonai himself.

Meanwhile, Brother had very real functions at home. It was his home in the special sense that everything done there was in a way pointed at him. It was the three women's house to manage entirely; where the money ran short they had to make up for it by better managing. From certain little colloquies that passed over my head there were surely problems of supply, and here Aunt Beck was queen, with the sisters coming up ever more staunchly in their roles. Plump, passive Nita, greedy Nita, was a first-class cook, if on the sweetish side. Back in Virginia she might not have worked; here she made abortive efforts to run a typing agency—by certain family signs unprofitably.

Nor had Katie's job propelled her altogether out of the home. By what commuting struggles I never knew, she arrived at odd hours, whey-faced but true—and I had seen her give Beck money. Even so—and though Beck tried to baby her: "Put up your feet, dollin' "—she helped before mealtime and collaborated on Nita's pretty table settings, which appeared like artwork three times a day. Brother was merely called to table. What then did Aaron do—and quite successfully?

In his father's absence he kept up the tribal conformation of the house and the family, a complicated matter that I understood instinctively, both by home example and because I was female. At home (where my grandmother, married in 1852 to a man old enough to have been recorded "elder" of the earliest Richmond synagogue in 1832, would at her death be already a widow of some forty to fifty years' duration), we were much more of a matriarchy, if one in decline. There my father was the good provider and never prodigal youngest son except perhaps in his forays with women, though these had always been

effected at a distance from his mother's house and were
abandoned without a doubt at the time of his late marriage
to my mother. Meanwhile, on the domestic side, he was
overwhelmed by dependent women—or would have been,
had not the amenities tendered him as boss Lord been as
strictly kept there as these were at the Pyles'.

Aaron, then a slight, pleasant young man in his twenties, must have had some piffling job that would lead to the
small printing business he would commute to the city to
until his death in harness—on the Manhattan subway—
in his hardy eighties. That summer at Port he could not yet
have been the provider, but there was hope. In the mean-
time—which was where he gave the appearance of
being—he was served first and with his favorite foods, and
had no household responsibilities as far as I could see, even
to the gardening, which belonged to Beck. All evenings
and weekends, and some afternoons, he was at leisure, no
doubt for girls, but also, as I saw more at firsthand, for
hunting and fishing. Although Long Island was more rural
then, my guess is that the rabbits Aaron sometimes brought
home came from local hutches. But what of the quail—
did that come from some acquaintance living on land the
Northern equivalent of a Shirley? Possibly, for though we
were city people now, I was used to hearing of the social
semblances, tricks, and even sly thefts that came of living
nearer the land. Of say, hearing my father, who up North
couldn't hang a picture or string a bootlace, tell with glee
of how he poached gardens when a boy: "So there was this
melon hanging on the vine, prizewinner, ready for the

fair—and half a dozen starlings, ready to peck. So what could I do but take out my pocketknife?"

Anyway, whether or not Brother always shot the game, he supplied it. And he took me fishing once, like a somewhat younger uncle taking me for a walk.

We fished for young blues—stripers, did they call them?—and in milksop fashion, on a Sunday afternoon, off the club dock. Yet I was feeling more Southern than I had in a long time. School had long since doused my diphthongs in the taut New York whine, but here in Port I had half got them back.

On either side of the porch at the Pyles were, as Aunt Beck teased me, the jelly bushes; in the kitchen the actual syrup might be aboil, much like the talk on the "veranda," which was what the lowliest sideporch might at any moment turn into. There the "expressions"—my father's word for idiom—flowed into my ear in a sugar stream that melted like cotton candy, before one could taste or interpret them, and tasks were thrust into a young hand without fuss or stricture: "Here, li'l ole Hot-tenz, he'p pop these lima beans." I had had a hard time with the limas. "Soft as a baby's behind, that's why."

Beck's voice was old and granular, although she must then have been still in her fifties. She wore her hair in a knot on top of her head, and makeup had never touched her, nor Katie either. Blondish Nita powdered her nose, and once, in her bedroom, while I was watching her do it and just about to ask her why only the nose, she had said, "Hush. Here comes Ayron." He would only pass by, and never enter unless invited. In that small house, room etiquette was strictly observed. But the facepowder, if noticed, would not be approved. And he would have his way.

"Katie likes to fish," I said to him, that day at the dock. "But she seldom gets the chance." I was beginning to champion her, in my head.

"Don't know what we'd do without Katie. My older sister is a fine girl."

He was teaching me to fling up my line in an arc over my head and forward, the hook dropping on a plumb line into the water. If I had a nibble, I was to fling up the line in the same arc, but backward, slamming my catch on the dock behind me. We sat on the edge of the dock, dangling our legs, I in Sunday costume, at which to my surprise Beck had not scolded, as would have happened at home— though if any female there had ever fished, even back in Richmond, it was never recalled.

"Keep your elbow close to those skinny ribs of yours," Aaron said. Like all the Pyles, he was a tease. "And like shuck your hand, at the wrist. Don't shuck the whole hand, a course. Couldn't bring you home to Beck in that pickle. Have to drown you right here, hair bow and all."

"Hush, yew," I said.

Freestyle or not, I caught fish after fish. Aaron caught nothing.

—Sometimes I think that people who live by memory as much as I do should be shot. Early. It's too delaying. Sometimes one brings up a pearl, yet must wait forty, fifty years for it. We won't hear from Katie on this until she is eighty-three. At which point she will explain everything, except what it is that I most want to know—

Anyway, at that moment, a young man about Aaron's age came from behind us, strolling down the dock arm in arm with a girl. If we had been fishing hard, with our backs curved toward the water, we wouldn't have seen them, but Aaron, who had given up his own line in mock despair, was taking my latest catch off the hook, and I was totaling the wriggling blues in the pail. I caught a sidelong flash of the young woman because her dress was maroon, not a summer color. Her hair, dark as mine, was sculptured down her back the way I would want to do, if ever I wanted to hang that way on a man's arm instead of catching blues.

"Hi, Aaron."

"Hi, Edward."

"Who's your cute partner?"

I kept my eye on my line. I knew I was being used. This Edward was really speaking at his girl. And I knew I wasn't cute. But at my age people spoke through you and out the other side. Or thought they did. My side at this minute was the fish. And the almost clear water that was sending me gift after gift.

"My young cousin from *New* York. She's teaching me to fish."

"Teaching Aaron Pyle?"

"I haven't caught a thing. Not since she started."

"Maybe she could give me some pointers," the Edward voice said.

"You seem to be doing right well." Aaron's speech was always mild but his hand on my elbow was tight. If he didn't watch out he'd destroy my rhythm. "May I know who your friend is?"

"Miss Myra Manheimer, meet Aaron Pyle, our near neighbor. Myra's a kind of cousin. We grew up together. At Woodmere High School. Before she moved to the city. And we moved here."

"Oh, I think Port Washington is lovely."

If she didn't know yet not to say the Washington, she hadn't been here long.

"Just come?" Aaron said.

"Oh, I plan to be here a lot."

"And welcome," Aaron said. But his voice was on its high horse, as any Southerner could hear.

"Hope to meet your sisters, Air-on," the Myra voice said, cool.

As usual the voices above my head were exchanging on some level I wasn't privy to. But today none of them was privy to what the underwaters were telling me. My arm ached with the weight of it, although if a striper weighs four ounces it is doing well.

"I have a nibble," I whispered, praying I wouldn't spook it.

"Hang on to it," Aaron said. He had released my elbow. I could tell he wasn't looking down at me. "Or no—maybe let it go."

I couldn't. I arc'ed the line. Backward, and over my head.

The fish slapped down the middle of the maroon dress. A short-sleeved square shift, silky with city confidence. We would call it art deco now. A pearl. Maybe it wasn't ruined forever; maybe the hook hadn't caught. Many's the time I'll see it, but I'll never know.

Aaron didn't begin to chuckle until the two of them had vanished toward the clubhouse. "Oh, hon'," he said when he'd finished a second burst. "Oh, hon'."

"I didn't mean to," I said. "Truly. My hand shucked all of itself. I was only thinking of the fish."

"Keep thinking so, hon'—you'll do all right. And no need to say anything about it at home." His face, scooped longer in the chin than Katie's, said I wasn't to.

The live fish in the pail made me uneasy, bumping their mouths first on one side then the other, like goldfish did in their bowls. "Let's throw 'em back, shouldn't I?"

"You have a real instinct. I'm right proud of you. Ordinarily, yes, they'd be too small to keep. But not tonight. Beck is expecting them."

Beck fried them up without a word. My heart beat with love for my Southern relatives. If they had been loud in appreciation I would have hated them. They knew the fish were not yet table fish. They simply smacked their lips and smiled. All except Nita, who apparently had spent all the afternoon in the good dress she'd worn to teach Sunday School and kept asking who all had been at the club.

When I left Port, Beck said: "Come back anytime, you rascal."

"Oh, thank you, Aunt Beck. Thank you kindly."

Her eyes squinched merrily. "That's colored talk, you little monkey. Wherever'd you pick that up, up here?"

"Oh—" We always had help in the house. The Pyles didn't. I didn't like to say but didn't know how to get out of it—a state in which I spent much of my time. "From *die Schwarze*, I guess."

"Hmmph." I could tell she didn't like that expression either. But she pressed me to her chest anyhow, a surface ample but hard, capaciously breathing. I had never felt a chest like it—always receiving, squared off down to the bone. "Pore little monkey." No tape could spell the way she said "poor." The minute she said it, I saw myself in the pail. All of us.

I left college, degree in hand. Left home to work and have my own apartment. Left work to marry, to have a family, and to live in many "out-of-town" places, none of them speaking in any of my accents, my own speech floundering unreliably along the way. I did not know myself, so I was what I heard, if with a core of obstinacy below the larynx. One day this stubbornness would move my writing arm to bypass my tongue and connect with my head, and ultimately with my life, but it hadn't happened yet. During those same pre-years, the household of my childhood, up to then numbering only four at the center but vastly accommodating, had swelled for a final time with the increments of war.

As my father went bond for as many refugees from Hitler as he could afford to sponsor, most of them tenuously related to my mother through the half-brother, Sigmund, who until then had scarcely paid his emigré sister any mind, our dining room filled with their tales of former grandeur and with their pudding handshakes. We heard of Onkel Sigmund's house in Berlin, where the dining salon had been walled in red tapestry, of his son's ski hut in the Dolomites, and of how Onkel himself, former head of General Motors for Germany and owner of a car the twin of Von Hindenburg's, had got used to being mistaken for the old Minister, sometimes even opening its window and graciously accepting the plaudits of the crowd. We heard from his son the skier, whose exact cousinship confounded me— what would the son of a step-uncle be to me?—that our party manners were low here; in their drawing rooms, each time a guest entered, the whole company turned and acknowledged him.

I was too young to give them full credit for the trauma they had suffered even though their skins were safe, but watched entranced as they collided with my Southern family and each side gradually became aware that it was being condescended to.

Who knows what this forced alliance might have brought about, if the economy had not intervened? Bitterly disappointed that my father could not establish them in businesses suited to their station—for we were still feeling the effects of the Depression, and although when young he had rebounded from an ancient war, he was too old now to profiteer from this one—the new "Germans" took what he could offer and bowed themselves out. Leaving me with the lesson one balks at learning—that people as people are often distinct from the tragedies or injustices that they may suffer, and not always in tune with them.

One thing our household had been in harmony with—time. Indeed, by virtue of our double heritage we seemed to live under a double dose of it. As Jews, we possessed the biblical sense of time according to the Old Testament, that confused bag of endlessly instructive verses telling us there was a time to do this, a time to do that, from sybarite hours in the gardens of the Song of Solomon to Ecclesiastes' final message of worn teeth and broken bowls. As Southerners, we were bound together by long, genealogical afternoons in which one had only to kiss to be cousins, and by the anecdotes that rose like hashish smoke from these long-burning histories. No wonder then that death, natural and unnatural, always took us by surprise.

My family went down like the *Lusitania*. What precipitated it was the death of my mother, at fifty-eight—not that young, but so long thought of as twenty-two or more years younger than the generation she had married into, and as wife to a man who at seventy had still had a mother, that her death seemed as untimely as if she were still a girl. Within the year my father, until then a healthy eighty-two-year-old who had looked sixty, dropped in her wake. Then only did it become clear to their left-behind retinue what had happened.

Not since my own childhood, during which my father had lost his two elder brothers and my grandmother her sons, had "anybody" died, until at ninety-seven, she had. After that only the brother-in-law, Uncle Clarence, had been lost, exiting as modestly as he had lived. For fifteen years or so the planetary arrangements of our little universe had gone on, as if its original cause, their matriarch, were still among them. As everybody, down to the last little subway-riding cousin, had expected it to. My father, holding up under the burden like a five-foot-eight Atlas, had never thought of absconding; my mother, cured of her breakdowns by the challenge of being her own mistress, no longer rebelled.

Only we young had defected, partly from circumstances (I at a distance and my brother in the service) and, as was intimated by the elders any time we could get there, also from the notorious unfaithfulness of youth. How could they know that even to the neglectful, the parent house is always there to be gravitated to, in the mind? Even the real cousins, those unreliables, now and then gave evidence of that—Grace, Flora and Clarence's daughter, steaming in from her unsuccessful marriage in Syracuse to its proper home audience, or even one of Belle's reprobate girls, Gertrude-Pat, who, bumping into me from behind the dresses in a department store, both of us women now, said hungrily from whatever new fastness of creed, "Uncle Joe's? Is it still there?"

But now there was no meeting place, come sewing-circle time, or of a weekday evening, or for Sunday's chicken fricassee. With perhaps the promise, for some, of a little cash thrust in the palm, or at least a bottle of scent from the family factory. There was no place to go. Simple as that. A whole entourage had died.

"You couldn't keep it up, maybe, could you?" old Cousin Martha Jacoby from Newark, the little old seam-stress with the tic, said wistfully, thrusting her whole inex-perienced and needy life at me so pitiably that, arrived though I had from six hundred miles away, two small-fry to care for and not much money, I thought for a moment that I could do so—that I must.

Behind me all the old familiar faces, as the song said, were massed up at me as if they, too, half believed I could, although we were in the bedroom now, not the living room—with all the secretive dresser drawers and crammed closets open at last to the curious, and not one of my childhood's viewing corners left.

"They here for the pickin's," my father's black maid had said, as they all filtered in the week after his funeral. After my mother's death he had gone back to black servants. She was a recent one; she scarcely knew us. But she knew the picture, *die Schwarze*, as from the Bronx on they always had, she even alerting me that the Germans, keeping up our divisions even in condolence—and in a memento seeking of drawers guaranteed to have been, as they virtuously said, my mother's only—had come in advance, the day before.

Those present no longer looked like a planetary arrangement, these calico-on-a-stick aunties and Punchinellos of the dining table who had chirped me toward adulthood and chucked my school days under the chin. Taken together, they looked to me like one of those threatening Italian pictures without perspective, in which all the flat faces are ranged toward the one—whose gaze they will hold for life.

"Co'se, she cain't," a soft but strong voice said from the door, a voice that would never be in such a lineup. "How could she keep it up? For one thing, she lives away. And what would she be doing it faw!"

"It's the Pyle girl," I hear a spinstery voice say from among the female heads bent over the opened bureaus and cupboards in exact pecking order, the aunts in control of those upper drawers, which always seem to hold a woman's costumery for above the neck—here the combs and jewelry not good enough to be kept at the bank. Lesser cousins of the blood, like Martha, are prowling in the chest that still holds my mother's "materials," from dress-goods to bolts of damask never yet cut into napkins, to that ragbag of torn sparkle-stuffs from the 1920s, which had been glamour to me when I was at the age for dress-ups, and one day would be again. Some of the storage places I had never been allowed to pry to the back of, and I see how the death of a woman domestically—that is, aside from the trials of the body—is in the sight of all her panoply, open and awry.

Whosoever the grayish second voice had been, I hear its

hostility freshly also, now that I am of an age to understand the animus of the home women against those who venture out into the world, and I see how the men are absent from this part of death, how they never have to do what we are doing here.

"Yes—it's the Pyle girl," Katie says, smiling at me over their heads, for if she is still a girl, what am I? "Been on a case, hon'. Couldn't come before."

Over the intervening years I always knew how she was faring, and she of me and mine, but I had been living from city to city and in New York only intermittently, and she busy in her orbit, so we had not met.

She was forty-five by then and not much changed, merely no longer twice my age. Indeed we were nearer.

She in turn was now almost the age my mother would have been on the opening night of this account. While my mother, down her long trail from the smocked tot in the photo brought from Germany to her terminus at fifty-eight, can be any age memory chooses. And I am grown. Or had been, after the ship went down, until this moment. For after this, although we meet no more frequently, perhaps every other year, and at one period lose track of each other altogether, Katie will keep me in my childhood until the end of her life.

And I will grasp at the chance, as if I am sinking in a quagmire and pulling my savior toward me. Which is the true and everlasting stance of the mnemoniac.

Mneme is the Greek word for memory. There should be a word for extreme devotion to memory. As there are insomniacs, kleptomaniacs, so should there also be—mnemoniacs.

A word that we are coining between us here, she and I.

It is October 1981. She and I and my husband are in Port. Not Port Washington but Port Charlotte, Florida, where she and Nita went to live after Katie retired and they had finally sold the Long Island house. Or rather, Katie had sold it. For although this has never been expressed until today, I have somehow long known that after Solly died so many years ago, whatever the date—for Katie is over eighty now—the girl with the teacup eyes became the sole support of their house.

The house where we are now is after three days no longer a shock to me. Katie, the girl who shot over the acres of Shirley, the young woman who poulticed a war, and the slender old woman whose spirited elegance is her sole adornment—what is she doing in this yellow ranch box, model dwelling for the too safely retired, midway in a varicolored but all too similar row of the same? How has she come to it?

I am beginning to know. These few days I am being told everything. Not in extreme haste, but to a pattern. We are in the drama of the last dwelling place, where it seems to me the Chinese property men always present in our lives are bringing out the furnishings one by one.

"You look just the same," we say to each other with
passion, on meeting. I don't know how I look and for once
don't care. Here is the person who casts me back, into any
one of several distinct yet blending stages I can choose from
at will, yet experience all at once. If I came to think of any
family gathering of substance both as a kind of ritual
bath—in which that day's bathe echoes all the past ones—
and as a kind of memory picnicking, Katie is the sharer to
whom I will not have to explain. Here is the mentor, the
chuckler, whose ethic helped form me. Here is the person
who knows where I came from.

Although I increasingly kept in touch with her by phone
now, we hadn't seen each other since three years before,
when I had persuaded her to come North to visit us in
Saratoga, the summer after Aaron had died. Nita, her
remaining lifelong companion since the death of their
mother, had died a couple of years before Aaron, nursed
faithfully by Katie through a long siege of heart trouble.
Aaron and his family, a wife and grown daughter, she and
Nita had seen rarely, in their visits North to see doctors or
for Katie's class reunions. From hints chastely dropped and
quickly withdrawn, I could hear that there had been a
"situation" about money lent Aaron long ago and never
retrieved from his widow when Aaron's house was sold,
while her niece, his daughter, once Katie's cherished
"Joanie," now married and living in California, was never
heard from.

Through this screen I might also hear too suggestively
how to them Katie might have become, respectively, the

elder sister, sister-in-law, and aunt who was still trying to hold on to Aaron in the name of Beck, and to impose on his women standards of conduct from an unshared past that they would have found both dowdy and severe. I had had aunts like that. Although Katie would surely have been far less unbending than they, I could see how to any young niece growing up in Great Neck, only a few miles from old Port but an eon away, and farther still from Virginia, Katie would have seemed both too rigorous and no model to imitate. As for critic sisters-in-law, my mother, alas, had had those.

After Nita's death I had had no qualms about Katie's ability to live alone; she and her sister had quite apparently become as ingrained in the life of the second Port as they had been in the original. Katie, besides, had a network of telephone correspondents who rang her as regularly as I, who in her and my conversations were referred to like a cast of listeners-in, to whom I in turn was almost strenuously united across the air channels: Dr. Forrester, the woman doctor she had worked with and so revered; Dr. Siletsky of Great Neck—"almost like a son"—whose name I privately recorded in event of any problem that the Florida doctors, a sad lot by her report, should not handle; her friend Pearl, met once, to whom I sent yearly bulletins on the progress in our garden of her gift slip of bergamot. I had no doubt that I was a staple in their conversations with Katie as well. None were from the South, but Katie, with a dulcet expro-priation whose style I surely recognized, was cousining us all close. Meanwhile, when I phoned on holidays I would hear the sounds of company and her offhand "They know they can't expect Nita's cooking, but they come anyhow"—or else a mention of to whose house she was bespoke.

But when Aaron died, I pleaded with her to come North for a visit. He had been "Brother." Now she was lone as well as alone; she was the last, and that was different. I was beginning to know how that would be. My own younger brother was very much alive, but he had come almost too late for the crowded firmament I had been born into, and as the first male heir in the family since my father, he had been in his own orbit from the start. Remembrance of a family who, except for my father, he had deemed negligible seemed to bother him—although, taken young into my father's business world of the greats in the perfume industry, he could be elegiac enough there. Jessica, for years an aging recluse, had become more or less my charge, managed from a distance as I could. I was the last for her, from our mutual world. Katie would be mine.

During the week she was with us up North I had coddled her as if she was indeed an artifact, heaping her bed with the best old patchwork, bringing her breakfast on a tray. Her wanness on arrival had warranted it; now she blushed with attention. "You're babying me, hon'," she said one morning that I recall with the gratitude one has for having been able to pay out love in time. She was lying happily whelmed under the best embroidered sheets, and though

the coverlet, twined with blue morning glories infinitesi-
mally worked by members of my husband's family, had
nothing to do with her except to match the durable blue
of her eyes, she understood the tribute. In the world
we had shared on my mother's side, embroidery was
heraldry, too.

"Nobody's babied you for years. I mean to try."

The eyes widened, but held back in the old way. I knew
she was thinking of Beck, and I marveled at how old
women could dream of their mothers.

A spa summer can seem too shallow for the tragic virtues
but is prime for entertaining in the old-fashioned way.
Between Saratoga's horses, waters, galas, and the pecu-
liarities of the institutional estate my husband ran and at
the far end of which we ourselves lived—gardens on and
on behind the huge trees, woodchucks who plodded the
landscape as slowly as tamed cub bears, in the distance a
mansion house, and even, scattered over the fields, hired
hands who from afar might not be perceived to be mostly
white—we might qualify to be Shirley, almost.

I hadn't mentioned this until Virgil Thomson came up
to be our other houseguest. I had been sure he and Katie
would get on, and so they had. Born in Missouri, he had
still other qualifications. In spite of his vaster abilities, they
had the same manner, the same Southern love of gather-
ings, and the same humorous zest. So, one eve, when
through the glass wall of the sitting room we saw Woodchuck, the huge one who lived under my studio across the
lawn, actually come out on its stone step and survey his

domain, I said, "Katie, get your gun"—and from then on Virgil and she swapped stories, for he, too, had known the likes of Shirley.

One evening he said to me, out of her hearing, "I adore your cousin."

I think of her response when I told her this as more Southern than I could ever approach. The twinkle she said it with bridged all gaps—and was meant to.

"He's home folks."

But in the succeeding summers, though well enough except for abiding cervical pain, she had not come, saying that she was no longer of an age to stir from home. So that fall, we came to see her.

Always slight, she had become one of those gaunt old women in whom, as approaching death refines, one can see both the girl they were and their genealogy. Her bones and jawline were nothing like Beck's, yet as she plucked a big lemon from the tree in her front yard and gave it to us, or her hands knuckled over the chicken stew she insisted on making or plashed at the kitchen drainboard, I could feel her mother behind her and relearn the lesson the years keep trying to teach me—that the in-and-out flirt of the genes in family-descended flesh is elusive and wonderful.

"I must smell like a chicken," she said, laughing. "I eat so much of it. The skeleton shrinks with age, you know, and my bridge no longer fits the jawbone."

As always when she referred to medical facts her tone was professional; a skeleton was "the" even when it was hers.

HORTENSE CALISHER

The laugh was still silvery. "But at eighty-three, why bother?" She had become slightly prideful of her years, as old people do. But her doing this only reminded me how long it had taken her to become unoriginal. "Besides, I don't approve of the dentistry down here."

Her face darkened, as I noted it had now and then begun to do, as if age was permitting her to release certain shadows she had hitherto kept back.

Her gaze scanned the tiny living room, a box as conformist as Florida could show and barely able to contain even the further reduced detritus of the Pyles. In a corner one could not call far, the china closet. On the only full-length wall, a combination breakfront, bookcase, sideboard, and general repository, which every Virginia household of us had once had. Walnut looks dingy in Florida, and mahogany sweats. The television, once located in front of the big straight-backed armchair that Katie sat in nightly, her neck swathed in hot compresses, was now pushed aside; except for the news and the weather, she said, she was no devotee of the tube. A matching armchair was pushed to the wall, beside it. Her glance now settled there. "Nita loved chicken," she said.

After Nita's death, Katie had sent North to me Nita's silver-backed dresser set, its comb, brush, and mirror initialed *RAP* in the gracefully intertwined scrolling of the late teens of this century. So, Anita would have been her middle name. I never asked for sure, although I had thanked Katie with warmth, for I knew what had prompted the gesture—that I was worthy of a relic of Sister, of Katie's own honored dead. When Katie had come to Saratoga, the dresser set had been displayed, otherwise not.

I had never liked Nita, because of the sense of not being used enough that was always about her, or for her fondant plumpness, as from too much sweet cuisine and sex unsatisfied, and above all for the dreadful craftwork that flowed from her like the issue of all this, both a coy assertion of femininity all too Southern and a contradiction to the good plain living and linen at Port. Once, on a visit to us in New York, she had presented me with a crocheted cover for toilet paper, scabbed with pink wool roses and shaped to the roll of paper already inside. "For that extra roll to keep in the bathroom, hon'," Katie had said, her mouth quirking, when she saw I didn't know what it was.

Above all—I knew now—I had disliked Nita for her dependency on Katie. Altogether, Rachel Anita had been too gracefully entwined. Yet I also knew I must now mention her. I followed Katie's glance, to the television set.

"Must have been a siege," I said.

"It was." I saw her relief—in that my manners had proven what they should be. This could only mean that my feelings on Sister had been known to her all along. "Two and a half years. In and out of oxygen. I kept her here; she hated the hospital. I cared for Sister myself. She couldn't tolerate anybody else." Was there a trace in her voice of that elegiac we use when we appropriate the dead for our own sore needs? "She died in my awms, Hot-tense."

Was there a trace, too, of self-satisfaction at one's own virtue, which I had never heard from Katie Pyle before? Yes, there was. But didn't one need that—was I, too, beginning to feel?—in order to round out things to the seemly, an adjective, or was it adverb, well describing what Katie and I had been brought up to be?

I had seen such lifted chins elsewhere, on platforms, where people are awarded their just deserts. But it can happen privately, where there is family to watch.

"And me?" I said. "I more or less began in those arms, didn't I?"

"When you were born? Aw, no. Your daddy wouldn't let anybody with a germ within yards, 'cept the doctor and the nurse." She giggled. The chuckle had reverted to her own age back then. "But I wasn't far. Hattie—your mother—had us all to luncheon that very day. The whole shebang. You were late in coming, and she said that if anything could help bring on her pains it would be that."

My mother had had humor. But as with her cookery, her audience had never given her credit for it. Nor had I, until after her death.

"They all came like a shot," Katie said. "You know your mother's meals, when she made up her mind to them. Your aunts Mamie and Flora, the sisters-in-law even, which wasn't usual. No men except Uncle Clarence. Anyway, when her pains did begin, your father should have sent them all home, but he was so upset he didn't. Hattie was furious when she heard about it later. 'Can't I even give birth in privacy?' she said. But your father was half out of his mind. Later on I had my fill of expectant fathers. But I never in my life saw one take on so as Uncle Joe. Your aunts did suggest he go in and sit with his mother— but he had the sense to refuse that."

I burst out laughing. "What nasties they could be. We forget, you know, that he was their younger brother."

I had meanwhile made what I had thought to be a final peace with my mother's difficult personality nearly forty years before, in almost the first story I wrote, but this even more belated sense of her outrage made it complete. I felt the peace not of justice rendered merely, but of an intimacy I had never felt before. After all, I had been there.

"Even the sisters-in-law were there, eh? Even Belle?" That most romantic of my "aunts"—that white-haired but young looking and stylish lovely who had once, when I was perhaps nine, taken me to lunch in a chic restaurant with a balcony, where other women like her were smoking cigarettes. The same aunt who, once a widow, would turn her girls into Christians and disappear into a feud.

"No, not Belle. She was never around for any fuss. Whatever made you remember her?"

I heard that jealous severity, now more marked, but in truth long since taken for granted by me as what even a person as gentle and fair as Katie might not escape—the judgmental austerity of women who went much to synagogue. On their own. Often in place of their brothers, or of the women their brothers tended to marry. Often even as surrogates, in a small way, for their fathers. Women who find in these devotions that ethic, almost more male than male, of women who could have been—who could never be—rabbis. I knew a writer like that, who was almost more religious than God, and certainly more severe. Sometimes, though I didn't go to synagogue except in nostalgia, I heard that ethic in myself.

"But I was there," Katie said now, sunny and natural again. "The other cousins did leave, but I stayed on. I was fifteen and already wanting hard to be a nurse. So, you know what I did? You'll never guess."

"How can I?" It's not every grandmother who can hear for the first time a firsthand account of her own natal day, and one that sounds gratifyingly close to a royal accouchement.

"I made your father a mint julep."

"One of Ayron's?" When Aaron was in his eighties and still going briskly to business on the train from Great Neck, my husband and I had visited him and his wife, Leona, there and had been served one of those. It wasn't the frost on the silver cup or even the mint that made the real julep, Aaron told us. Or even the crushed ice. All that, he implied, was just Southern sweet talk—even Southern fakery—without the one and only secret ingredient. Many people had pleaded for the recipe, he said. I had pleaded: "Oh, Ayron, give it me." By his blink I knew I had swallowed the bait. "Double the bourbon," he'd said.

Katie blinked now. "Except for those old Midol pills for menstrual cramp, it was the only prescription I knew."

After we'd howled over that I said, "Well, you saved me, later."

And finally she admitted it.

"I've never been sorry."

The town of Port Charlotte is a senior citizens' precinct, and a good or bad dream, according to your lights. The Senior Citizens Center, one of the largest in Florida and in the nation, has room after room replete with the stately activity of "the golden years" and with what one begins to think of as their scrollwork: all the collections, some in memory of their owners, of china, shells, and dolls gathered on cruise travel, as well as the handicrafts of the living—woollies and watercolors and objects for uses oddly peripheral to honest day-to-day hours, and of an obsessively miniature deftness that sadly shows up the poor materials, the latter, yes, much flecked or woven or sealing-waxed with gold.

In Port Charlotte and its environs, medical advertisements—for doctors, clinics, hospitals, insurances—are everywhere on the roads and posters, and in the handout literature. The town is a billboard for age. Even in the supermarkets, where large sections cater to the sugarless and the salt-free, but most clearly in the favored restaurants, where the dining hour is early and the menus are easy on the dentures, this Port knows who is boss here. If in Hollywood the skin lesions made by time are to be hidden like one's crimes, here the liver spot is worn like a medal. Nor does age here go about in black cerements. Absolved from wool, old age in the Sunbelt walks in pastel: lime green and dusty rose or blinding white, topped with the sporting cap or straw skimmer or floppy picture-hat, all underwritten by running shoes. There are blondes among the old women here, but not like those in Miami; the decent rinses here sometimes even fade toward an acknowledged gray. No children appeared on the streets of houses anywhere near Katie's, but in the following days I would see some in the elaborately fancified mall one got to over a drawbridge not too many miles away.

Katie's neighbors were known to her within a radius of several blocks.

"Well, you always made friends," I said.

"Ye-es," she said. "But hon', you know my *friends* phone in from everywhere." I saw that although we were not to talk about it further, I was meant to understand the emphasis.

Twice we did go out to a neighbor's for dinner. The first time we went to the house of an elderly couple who though unmarried were living together in the man's house. "They're not marrying because of their respective children," Katie said offhandedly.

"We're a long way from Martin Freeman, aren't we?" I said, recalling Martin's mistress, whose status in our house, even when accepted, had been hushed.

"Down here we're just practical," Katie said, which seemed to be the general attitude of the company. The second time, we went to an early pre–Friday night service casserole dinner, the donors all women, in a house larger than most and comfortably masculine. The host, a spritely widower named Clayton, and lovingly called "Clay," clearly functioned in all propriety as group husband, if solely in the matters of advice on cars, income-tax, house repairs—and perhaps walks. Indeed, as he accepted an extra gift of two straw mats the donor had that morning braided, and in spite of the giver's remark—"I saw you had a white spot on Millie's nice table"—placed them on a shelf with other wild-angled, pumpkin-colored contributions, he appeared to be a kind of communal Uncle Clarence. He told my husband with a twinkle that he cleared off that shelf once a month. "In favor of my own hobby."

And what was that?

"Space."

Katie, watching me sharply as I took in all this sociology, said: "When Clay flies his airplane models around the room, I reach for my beekeeper's hat."

"Oh, do you keep bees?" a woman said.

From across the room Katie glinted at me. Only the room had changed. In that long ago family room across which Southern locutions had whizzed like those tiny, bunched firecrackers even children were allowed to ignite, she wouldn't have been challenged—although there had been some phrases I had accepted without ever knowing

their root meaning, and many now would sound anti-
quated anywhere.

"It's an old Southern expression," I said. "Actually, I
never saw a picture of such a hat until the other day. Listed
in some catalogue, maybe Bean's."

"Veiled, those hats are," Katie said, laughing. "No, we
never had them, even in Richmond. But I saw them down
home, once." She sent me another glance—enlisting me
to help her sustain that memory of Shirley of which,
though I could never share it, I had heard. "We'd look right
funny in your living room, Clay. But maybe I ought to get
you one. For that shelf."

"Katie keeps us all up to the mark," Clay said. But there
was no venom in it. Rather, he might be showing a preference, for someone who, among these soft widows, seemed
more single than spinster, and as spritely as he.

As we left, three or four intimates were chatting over
their prearranged system of alerts, in case of emergency.

"That must be reassuring," I said to Katie as we walked
on to the synagogue. She gave me a quizzical look. When
had she ever needed to be reassured? The hat she had put
on to go to evening service sat straight on her head, just
schoolmarmish enough to be without era. Her gray hair,
pinned up as she had always worn it, still had fairish streaks
out of no bottle but Time's, and her skin was still fine-
pored. "Nita loved it here," she said.

The services were held in a big, bright room walled with
very new, yellowish wood, much like a room in a parish
house.

"They just did it over," Katie murmured. When she looked dissatisfied her face drooped. Indeed, except for its pulpit, the place didn't look in any way blessed.

"So glad you could come to temple," one of the lady greeters said to us—and Katie's look held. Disappointment was more the word for it. I knew she did not approve of the term "temple," as being a poor substitute for the austerely traditional "synagogue." Her petulance rather resembled my father's higher-keyed irritability—in the family called "flying off the handle, Joe is," and always excused as being directed toward high concerns. Yet I could see how this relaxed looking, very Floridian congregation might view her—as one of those elderly women who cling to all congregations, and are always looking back. "Miss Pyle is one of our stalwarts," the young rabbi said.

During the service, several women came up to the pulpit at intervals, to read the lesson or read the responses. We had hit the monthly night when this innovation was now routine. Katie seemed amused. One woman's disquisition had been longer, learned, and delivered in piercingly nasal rabbinical style. This woman was indeed a real scholar, Katie said. "The others? Well—you know why they want to." Had she ever been requested to take part in the service? "Me? They know right well I wouldn't."

I thought of Brother, and of how far the women briefly up there on the pulpit were really allowed to go. Into the dogma of the Talmud if they had a taste for it. How far beyond? Could they serve in the early-morning assembling of the daily *minyan,* for instance—the sum of men required to be present for the start of a service? Might a woman be counted in there?

In the social hour afterwards, those who came up to be introduced, men and women both, nearly always told us where they had come from "before," exactly like emigrés. Although, unlike those who had streamed into my father's house, they were not refugees, they too seemed to be similarly divided, into those who by retiring "here" had risen in their own estimation and in actual class, and those who knew they had suffered a decline in their society and their tastes. When home-baked cookies were offered, Katie refused them, and indeed though they were soft enough to the gum they were not very good.

That night she apologized again for the meal she however had insisted on cooking, with assistance refused. I tried to measure whether her refusal was merely part of that hospitality, so familiar to me, which liked to declare to a guest, "Y'all stay right where you are!" Or did it come from an older person's ever-present fear that autonomy itself was draining away? I decided it was both—and ended up confronting how much my upbringing had taught me about the old.

"Rachel became a great cook after Mahma died," she said, serving us. "People fell over themselves to come here. But you'll have to make do with me."

Again I had a strong sense of her as a nurse, dealing year after year with situations where there was no time for vanity. Or for flattery? Over the years before she became a supervisor, Katie had now and then been persuaded to take on a case as night nurse, often of someone she knew personally, often terminal. What had it been like to sit alone night after night with the sense of your own inner credit only, and to see that credit vanish each time you shut the door on death?

" 'Cept Rachel always cooked too much," she said, with a reminiscent smile. "She was never happier than when the leftovers were spilling out the back door. I can't tell you how many second-night dinners we had to ask people back to, those last years. But she loved it."

"We didn't come here for your cooking, Katie." And even to her, home must be better than the restaurants, where the waitresses were as coy as social workers in their special recognitions of the old folks, and at the salad table one could have seconds of watery greens and macaroni and cottage cottage cottage cheese.

"I know."

"And 'home is always preferable.' "

We exchanged smiles at this phrase of my father's, that belle epoque gourmet who, after marriage, had settled into home fare like one of those great chefs who in their prime verge ever closer to the simples learned at mother's knee.

At least the china closet was here. For Katie, that is. Why, in this mean little house, should I be thinking of Shirley? Was it wrong then, after all, for age to be boss of itself and us—or only for age to be separate?

The chicken was a great-boned fowl cut into pieces, porridge-colored from steam. In effect I knew who had cooked it, even though I had seen Katie buy the pinkish packet at the supermarket. Beck had caught one of their two hens once and slaughtered it, the only time I had ever seen that done. Muttering, as she singed it and let me pick off the last pinfeathers from the wing tip with a tweezer, that it had ought to be hung, but that there was nothing else "handy" in the house. And Sol was coming home.

I was hazy about just when Beck had died, years after my own parents, at any rate, and probably during the 1950s, when I was at times out of the country, or far from the Eastern seaboard.

"Had Beck ever planned to come to Florida with you?"

"Mahma? She'd have cut her throat if she had known we were ever to sell Po-ut."

I'd forgotten Southern exaggeration, whereby you would "strangle your own mother" or "as soon put your sister down a well" before you would—what? Ruin good eggnog with cinnamon. Or drink Scotch, with or without ginger ale. Or wear an unmanly wristwatch—among the older men called "one of those." Or not wear a watch. It struck me now how many of these outsize statements had been couched in terms of family mayhem. Again I saw that hen whose neck Beck's hands had wrung and then severed—"a wrung chicken tastes better, dollin' "—running across the garden without its head. And I thought that Aunt Beck would have gone anywhere in the world Katie asked her to.

"No—but what Mahma loved was travelin'. And visitin'—my! After I bought a car you know how we did. If Nita'd ever learned to drive we could have done more."

Yes, I knew how they did. In the days when we and our

children, returned Eastward, were also living "on the shore"—of the Hudson River, not the Sound—and so by car only some sixty miles each way, the Pyles had come to visit us for the day. I had explained to the children that it would literally be for the day, and how it would probably be.

They would no doubt arrive for lunch—the three Pyles. "Three ladies," I'd said. I had lightly described them, keeping back what bias I could—but love will out, and no doubt it had. "It'll be a real sit-down lunch, with a lot of talk. And many stories," I'd said, as a lure.

Because of all the elderly deaths, my children had missed out on my side of the family altogether, and because of distance hadn't had enough natural flow from the other side. To my mind they had never been properly nested down in a clan. We and our friends, some of them writers, all of them vocal, had done what we could about stories, to which our younger boy and older girl were a permitted audience, whose comments, both sharp and entranced as only children can manage, were manna to their mother. The stories they heard had not been as genealogical as I could wish. Now I would be doing memory's job. I would be helping them to part of what I thought should be their place in life.

"And you two will have to be in attendance the whole day."

I was proud of that phrase; it gave exactly the tone. They had groaned at the prospect; with the whole river-and-village summer day open to them—why?

"For the honor of the family," I'd said, knowing that would intrigue them. "And because that is the way I was brought up," I'd added, grinning—on that subject I knew I was already the family bore.

"Yes, you know about my upbringing," I'd said, as severely as my always insecure adulthood could manage—because it was always placing itself on the side of the child. "But you've never experienced it."

The Pyles would certainly expect to be asked to dinner as well, before their long trek back, I said, and would take it kindly that the whole family would be there. If we wanted to be extra hospitable—I thought of Nita—we would also offer a light afternoon snack. "For which you two could opt out."

"Ice cream and cake?" They grinned back. Maybe they'd stay.

But why did I want it so much, one of them said, and the other answered: "To show us off."

That was true, and I duly blushed for it—now that I had children, blushes came easier. But since becoming a storyteller myself, I had learned that truth always intrigues. And although I had never fished since that once in Port, was maybe the best bait.

"Yes, I do enjoy that, more than you like. I promise to keep it down. But there's another reason I want you to be around."

Their pre-teen faces had been still apple-cheeked but already lengthening with pre-knowledge; could I burden those? "Because when we older ones"—should I say "go," or "die"? As a child I hated the euphemisms dealt me—only learning much later that drawing room comedy could be made of them. But that style of comedy is not deep enough for children.

"Because when we elders die, you will be our keepers," I said.

And all that livelong day the Pyles and we had the single, double, triple, quadruple, quintuple, and sextuple satisfactions that can crisscross a family, even if composed only of six dubiously related people and one like-minded, family-clogged father and spouse. I saw how the Pyles recognized even burgeoning memory-manners when they saw them, how touchingly they stretched their stories to provision this—and how thirstily they had needed this for themselves. I saw my children sink deep and gratefully into the genealogical texture. Alone in the kitchen, which, after giving them a look-see at my own husbandry I had forbidden the Pyles, I could hear only a satisfying family hum.

It can be pleasant to cook to the tune of that, and to provender it with old linen and spoons, maybe recognizable, too. At one moment, when the past became too poignant to be borne in company, I went into the bathroom and cried.

After the Pyles had gone, we all agreed that such a day was worth it, but almost too much.

The second time the Pyles had come to Grandview, that next summer, they hadn't telephoned, arriving unexpectedly on a midday that was to become notable in village lore—the day a zebra had blundered into a garden on the left bank of the Hudson, our garden. Later I had incorporated that incident into a story, "Mrs. Fay Dines on Zebra," that dealt with quite different people, among them a half-French heroine, Arietta Fay. But one sentence, after a description of the catching of the beast by the cops and the Hudson River Cowboy Association, had detailed as follows:

> At the height of it—children screaming, yokels gaping, three heated men hanging on ropes, the whole garden spiraling like a circus descended from the sky, and in the center of it all, the . . . striped, the incredible. . . . Arietta's eighty-five-year-old Cousin Beck from Port Washington, a once-a-year and always unheralded visitor, had steamed up the driveway in her ancient Lincoln, into the center of it all. "Oh, Cousine Beck," she'd stammered in French, she never knew why—"you find us a little *en déshabille*, we have us *un zebre*." And how Beck, taking one look, had eased her old limbs out of the car and grunted "Arietta, you *are* dependable. Just bring me a chair."

I had taken liberties. They were "unheralded" only that second time, which we couldn't know would be the last. And I wasn't Arietta. What I actually had said was: "Oh, Aunt Beck, you find us a little upset. We have a zebra in the garden." Beck may not have been quite eighty-five. The elders looked older in those days, often making almost a profession of it. But what she said in life and in the story were the same. She did not change.

"Yes, she did, didn't she. Love visiting," I said now. "Remember the day you all came to Grandview?" I am remembering that first time. How my daughter, long since dead, had said guiltily that she didn't like Nita. But liked the other two, in fact "loved" Aunt Beck—and why didn't we have more visiting days? How my son of eight, now a bearded man with his own daughters, had asked—where were the Pyle men?

What Katie remembers, chuckling, is the zebra day. "You got Mahma down to the life. And how she loved reading that story."

So, Beck had still been alive when I wrote it. Older people tend to disappear during one's absence. If the interval has been long, one accepts that, chary about asking the details, and guilty, too. It struck me that there was a lot I hadn't asked, about Beck. But age had its privileges—some grudgingly acceded to.

"Katie—was Beck's death sudden? I never knew."

"Naw, you didden." That tone, admonishing me from a central standard where manners were ethic, too—I have had it from her only once before: *What the devil did you think I went out to shoot?* Almost at once, though, her face quirks in its ever-jesting need to wish to be fair, to underscore the teasing we all get from life. "But by rights if you'd asked at the time I wouldn't have told you, hon'." A face that has quirked too much—when it is agonized, it can look like a frog's. "She just wore out. One day—she just wore out. And I was away on a case."

She reached for one of the hot compresses at her side,

pressed her face in and then slung the towel around her neck. "When you live with it you don't see it. But I should have. I'm a nurse."

I am not a nurse. But I am seeing it. In this sorry little room I am learning more than I want to know about the gossip of the old. When they pry the air thisaway, thataway like turkey gobblers following their beaks, they are weighing the long gossip to come—of themselves. I am feeling what it means when a person is beginning to disappear, carrying her history slung around her neck, and bearing that great box, the household that no one after her will so rightly know. Katie wants to hand hers over to me, in such proportion as she sees. But I have to help. I have to suck from her throat what she cannot expel herself.

"Katie. Was it your choice to come down here?"

For a swollen moment we are neither of us seeing these crackerbox walls that no china closet can turn into a real house loaded with time. Nor the roadways out there, chatty with advices on death. Nor those mountains of handicraft which, if carefully swapped with a neighbor, will keep both of you anchored to the sliding Florida earth. A nurse knows better, at least most of the time. And I have had a household from which the habitués have slid one by one.

"No. C'ose not. Sista chose it."

I have the distinct sensation that I have lanced a boil. Though I have had no medical training of any kind.

But now she is pleading with me. "Hon'—Rachel never had much."

So that's why I disliked her. As the rich dislike the poor.

"You were the elder, weren't you, Katie?"

"Nita was, by three years. But after a while, people didn't think so."

She says this equably, as an observed fact. I want to scoop up and tally the resentment she should have had.

"Because she was—so dependent on you. Didn't she have a typing agency once?"

"She went into debt over it. Mahma kept paying for it and didn't tell me. I'd just been made supervisor and couldn't get home much. My own head supervisor was a battle-axe." She made the kind of impish face that kids make behind the gym teacher's back. "Taught me how to be . . . And then I did get home, and found out. Mahma didn't have any more money. She'd been giving Ayron, too—he was just starting out. And she'd simply come to the end of what they had. . . . But all that was later, hon'."

"I remember! There was talk about it in the family. That was when you took on special cases—Sundays and holidays. And everybody except Daddy said you were too ambitious."

She chuckled. "So I was. To them."

"And that you would ruin your health."

"I 'most did. But then, you know, I'd been in the awmy, where health wasn't exactly"—she gave me a look, tender but critical. "Your family—I have to say it, dollin'. The whole lot of them on your father's side. Beck and I often said it. They were the healthiest hypochondriacs we ever saw."

And suddenly we begin to laugh and laugh. I can hear

our joint cackle almost separate from my half of it. Oh, what a release—and yes, a joining—for aren't I creeping up now, almost Katie's contemporary?

"It was just that they were always so *interested*," I gasped. "In what life could *do* to them."

As the laughter ebbs, she, too, leans back, released, and I think to myself, we could founder here; we could stay on memory's cute side, on the pawky side of the folklore, the kind that people love to buy—and why not? After all, hon'—you didn't die of that diphtheria.

But hadn't I been taught—only realizing now that my fond, fussy hypochondriacs had been the ones to teach me—that my early rescue gave me an extra obligation to life, to report on life?

We had forgotten the other chair. That's what a chair can do—look immanent. What a family of chairs we had been, each demanding that its history be kept up!

" 'Later,' you said, Katie. Later than what?"

"Oh—for Sista, I meant."

It comes slowly—why?

"She was a right pretty little thing, to start. Chubby always, but also—you know—fat oriented." There was a professional tinge to Katie's words now; after a period of mourning, those facts become memory, too. "How I tried to keep after her about the fat, but you knew Sista. Even those last months when the fat was around the heart like a—I saw the report, I made them show me it—but Rachel would say, 'I just cain't eat without butter to my bread.' "

I could hear the plaint, the intonation.

"I tried to restrain her—but it was all she had."

What about—men? I find I can't say it. We reserve a certain priggishness for our elders, for their own silly sake—even with a woman who can label her own skeleton. Or because where there is a Sista, there is the other sister—whose history is also lurking here?

"Rachel bore the brunt of our move North, you know. She was just that much older. Three years make a difference when you're a child. She stayed close to home. And Mahma made Port as much like down home as she could."

"So that was its charm for me. I never yet figured that."

Katie smiled almost condescendingly—as one does to a child.

"But she was attractive then? That should have helped. Weren't there ever any—?"

"Men?" Katie said comfortably, shifting the compress on her neck.

Why that gesture, so straightforward, should compel me to see her in another spectrum—I know full well. My generation had been schooled to measure what we do with the body as at once explanation of what we were or were not, and panacea for it. By era, Katie belonged to those women before me who mostly had not even exercised, much less carried their bodies in open and conscious demand. Now I was not so sure she belonged with them.

"That was when she wanted us to call her Nita." Katie stops short with that conciliatory shrug one gives when one is about to abuse someone else's confidence. "There was a young man—Hot-tense." Her voice drops into that soft rhythm in which we in the family told special stories, often about ourselves. "He was paying her attention. More than just a beau. Likely it would have come to a point. Then something happened. Mahma knew what it was and said it was nothing serious. Mahma had town connections; she said she had investigated—and Mahma never lied. She couldn't; that was her trouble. But Ayron took against the young man. And nobody could control my brother when he had a mind to be the man of the family."

Surely she had mourned him that summer she visited us—or mourned death—but the words are dry.

"The young man wanted to see Nita again, but Brother wouldn't have it. I was away then, too, but it wouldn't have made a difference. Because Mahma knuckled under. She crah'd when she told me of it. She had to let Brother be a man, she said. And Ayron had forbidden the other young man the house."

I could see Beck going the rounds of the town, maybe even to those not too well known to her, but doing what was done down home, where one's connections made gossip the best mediator. Staunchly setting out in the dress that could go anywhere. Waiting for Katie to come home, so she could cry. Waiting for Aaron to bring home the fish for dinner.

Then, quite without thinking on it, I made my connections—as any child of our long, female afternoons would—and clapped my hand to my mouth.

"What, hon'?" Katie has the rueful smile one wears when one has "told." "Something bit you?"

That, too, was what we had said among us, to sudden revelation.

"Nothing. Oh—Aaron and I went fishing once. At the club. And I disgraced myself. He ever say?" No need to mention it at home, he'd said.

"Hon'. You pee in your pants?"

"Good God, no. I was ten years old. I ruined a visiting girl's dress."

When I told her how come, she laughed again, of course, not noticing that this time I held back.

"They were a rich-looking young couple," I say, describing the dress. I didn't describe what the girl's companion wore, though I still remembered him perfectly—white flannel legs, blue blazer sharp-edged in the sun, brass buttons with anchors on them.

"Were those medals?" I'd asked Aaron as we walked home our catch. "No," he'd said, exploding again. "Far too many of them." Aaron himself had been wearing whatever fishermen wore, neat but unmemorable. Or what they had worn in Richmond maybe. When serious again his face was more rigid than Katie's, but his eyes had her blue. Walking along, jogging the pail, he'd dug me in the ribs again with his other hand, maybe too sharply. "Keep it dark about those two—remember? You and I just caught ourselves some fish." He saw my expression. "*You* caught them," he said.

"Wonder was that couple anyone from Port?" Katie said. To be from that Port was still an accolade.

Should I say? Death saves memory a lot of trouble.

"I had the impression that they were just down for the day."

So I left him in the archives, that young man, with his cousin Myra Manheimer, whom maybe he kissed, maybe he didn't. He came from the North, sure enough—this, and those buttons, were all Aaron really had against him. But why resurrect him now? There was no longer any call for him.

Note, though, how my cousin Katie and I both accepted without question the impressions of a ten-year-old child, half a century gone. In memory, all a family's children are smart.

"I was always making people laugh, those days," I said. "But you were all so good about those fish of mine. So small they should have been thrown back. But you ate them all, every one. I was so proud."

"Why, I remember that day." Katie sat up, the compress dripping in her hand, her mouth pursed in the peculiarly Southern mnemoniac way, the words so chewed one would be hard put to spell them: Waa-aah r'mimba would be accurate. "When you-all came home Ayron had words in the kitchen with Nita because she had makeup on, and her Sunday clothes. And me just off the train with my salary check, but Sunday, no way to cash. That's how I found out Mahma had come to the end of her savings. Here—give me that compress." She wound it around her neck with a savage flip she would never have used on a patient. "We ate those minnows of yours, hon', because Beck had nothing else in the house."

"That's a shock." I am only half joking. Childhood's triumphs are hard won—or mine were. And long cherished. "The thought of them warmed my pride for weeks."

Memory is a fish. A flashy something or nothing that can circle a pail twice. Or on and on. Memory is a bargaining—with what it has missed.

And something large, white, and shifty is missing here. A courtly man with a cane, in a white pongee suit. This is no time to be polite about that, with death breathing in our ears.

"And Sol—Beck said Sol might be coming home?"

She has finished with the compresses and dried her hands. Shapely at the nails but gaunt, they still move with a nurse's abstract competence, even toward a candy box. "Here. Have some nonpareils."

I've never known how to pronounce that word American-style and feel oddly grateful, though few may even know the term now.

"What was Uncle Solly's business? I never knew." I take one of the quarter-size chocolate rounds sprinkled with white. She munches on one. No, the teeth don't fit. One can see the animal taking over the human. That can be painful to watch.

"When Solly Pyle married Rebecca Boettigheimer he was a traveler, or supposed to be. Those days, men still had to travel in order to sell. Unless you owned a store."

I knew that picture. My grandfather had had such a store in Richmond; then came the War between the States. And later, a war between little commerce and big, as often happens after. "Between magnolias and merchandising" was the way my father said it; he'd wanted to be a poet, and alliteration was common in our house.

"Some of the men stayed on, and became department stores. And some of the men came North, like your father and mine." She's saying "min" now for "men." It's an old story.

We both lean forward. Those are the stories that have brought us to where we are.

"Beck only found out because of her wedding furniture, that Sol claimed was too heavy to move North yet, until we were sure of a big enough house. She'd thought it was going into storage. But Daddy had sold it to pay his debts down there. And the buyer-man came to our door."

Opposite us, the china closet has survived. Even Florida light can't always superannuate—one of our home words, too. I once asked Uncle Clarence what it meant, on one of our walks. "Being out of date," he said. "A condition common among people who come North." But, according to family estimate of a chap who worked in his brother-in-law's office, Clarence was not a successful man.

"Solly Pyle was a gambler," the teeth say with a click. "Let's have coffee now."

So we do. We both know when a story has ended—for the night. Whatever those teeth say, the eyes above have accepted it.

We are both quiet, maybe thinking about gamblers. Small businesses like my father's are gambles, but with a whole clan participating in the daily risk, and dependent on the kitty, the petty cash, the inventory—they become honorable.

"When my niece Joan was married I gave her the oldest family possession we had left over. Old blue china, eighteenth century, some of it. I understand she has it all over her house—but I never, never hear from her. Never. So I suppose she's all right. Doesn't need anything more. From me."

After a bit Katie leans forward. There's a certain formality in her manner. "Hon'—how about you? Are you all right?"

She means for money. Am I to be left something, in her disposals? These matters are not for sentiment. It is up to me to say.

I, too, lean forward. Whether we are talking about money or not—and I know we are, only the same words she has used will somehow express the intangible that I feel she will be leaving me.

"Yes, Katie. I'm all right."

On the way to bed she points to a small chest in the cubbyhole that is her dressing room. "Want you to have that anyway. Please take it when you go."

Little Dresden china plaques on it, lords and ladies playing shepherd and shepherdess. Cabriole stilt-legs—a chest a bride would love, or a child. Or an old woman. Not a trinket for men—and we already have too many of these in my house. I think of my granddaughters, still young enough so that when they're brides I may be gone. But something maybe should be left over, even from that far back. "It belongs in your room. I'll love to have it, some-day. But I don't want to denude you now."

I was wrong. She wanted to be denuded. They know when. When it is time.

The night after that we ate at the big mall, where I also bought an intricately cut parchment hat, tan colored, but made like those expandable paper Christmas bells, and in silhouette much like the charming "mushrooms" now being worn in all the British television series of the 1920s to 1940s, though I was not likely to wear it up home. "Keep it on awhile," Katie said, during coffee at home afterward. "You remind me of your mother in it."

Tonight I had been allowed to make the coffee; we were settling in. Though I would have to leave soon. The way younger people always do. We never really catch up.

"Wish I'd seen you in your nurse's hat."

"Cap, hon'. Yes, the Mt. Sinai cap—never will forget the day I earned it. Nothing like the dabs they wear today."

"Didn't know you trained at Mt. Sinai."

"Only way the family would let me train was if I was admitted there. I thought it was because they never expected me to qualify, the standards were so high. Hattie—your mother—told me the real reason years later—your mother loved a pun, you know. She said: 'They actually took counsel on you, Katie. They decided that if ever you set your cap at some doctor, it had better be a Jewish one.' "

I came to tally my mother's puns only after her death. Only recognizing then how complete and effective her tussle with our language had been—had had to be. Southerners are linguists by nature. People who drink "bourbon and branchwater" do so half listening to the lilt. She must have made up her mind that if English was to be our language supreme, with even her own child consigned to that view of it, then English was what she would conquer. My mother, too, had a tape in her head.

"You and Mother were close, weren't you."

"I had Beck, hon'—she had no one. Her own mother died when she was born. A stepmother—'til she came here. No women in your father's family she could be close to, even in age. You know all that. You wrote about it."

"Yet I never asked you about her—I don't know why."

"We have to figure these things out on our own."

How good it felt, it always felt, to find someone else brought up to do that. To find that these monastic cells we make for ourselves have a common wall.

"We got close when I came out of the awmy," Katie said. "Hattie and I."

When those stern hands of hers fisted, as they did now, they were like two quarters of chicken, each a breast-half with a second-joint thumb.

"Li'l old chickem bones, baby chickem bones," my

father, who couldn't sing, used to croon to me in my crib.
"Chickens are Jewish, aren't they," I said one day to the
Sunday table, rocking those gathered round the yellow
fricassee. "She means our beaks," an aunt who didn't have
one said. And maybe I did. But what I meant most was our
almost daily pore-to-pore sympathies with those fowl and
their bone-heaps. When the Holocaust came, I would
think again of them and us together, we staining the soup
with our yellow armbands, and jerking toward death without our heads.

"She was a German here, you know, all during the waw.
That took its toll."

"I know the neighbor women made it hard for her
because she knitted the German way."

In the American style, the incoming wool, held in the
right hand while that needle dives in for the next stitch, is
then looped around the point of that needle and drawn
through in a movement each time involving the entire
wrist, or even the arm. In the more economical German
method, the new wool, held to the left and close to the
chest, can be nudged in and out by the right-hand needle in
a mildly continuous motion that barely shifts either hand.

I used to think that such economies were merely part of
the obsessive lore of women, along with how you boiled
the said bones for stock. How surprised the Kaffee-Klatsch
must have been to find that their small, homely arts could
be politics. Or that calling sauerkraut "Liberty Cabbage"
was a not quite sufficient response.

"She had a stepbrother fighting on the German side.

She hadn't seen him since she came here at sixteen. But everybody knew. And do you know, when your father brought over him and his family during Hitler, they produced his picture in uniform, proud as proud?"

"Oh, even when I was a kid she asked me not to speak German anymore to our maid. When I was about six."

"Uh-*huh*. And do you know that you went to your father and said: 'So then can I go to Hebrew School like you did, instead?' "

"No! How extraordinary. That I don't remember that at all." I'd thought I knew all my language kinks.

"Your father didn't like to tell you—that girls didn't go. So he said he'd teach you. But your mother put the kibosh on it."

I smiled at the old word, never in the mouths of any I knew, except back then. Katie in her dark corner, wan under her pale hair, I in my paper hat—lightly, lightly in the small seagoing boat that is memory we're skimming toward youth.

"She must have been appalled. She didn't want to be Jewish."

That bitterness came back to me: how she had sneered at the name of a high school friend I had brought home, whose head of blond fuzz she had termed "kike hair." How when I went uncombed or unkempt I was accused of having the same.

"I know. You wrote about it."

Katie and I had never really talked much about my writing. As with many another writer's family, she seemed pleased that a member had gotten into print but felt no particular urge to engage with the books except for those that might chronicle the family itself—and this was fine with me. A friend had sent her the early stories, during the years when Katie and I were apart. Later, when we met again, those "family" tales had elicited a few chuckles on her side, but both of us were—I see now—uncharacteristically shy with one another there. I had been unable to write of my parents, or indeed of any of the others, until they were dead. She did not merely approve of this; she took it for granted in the old style—as the deference paid to one's elders. To her I'd been the "cute" little cousin—in the old sense of "acute"—who had sat on the bottom step of family conclaves and had "sure got everybody's number"— and she may not have been that wrong.

Now and then she would sometimes ask if I was "on a new one," in which case I must be "sure to send," but until the *Collected Stories* came out I never had—and not since. Because I truly felt she was not much of a reader, and because I had gone so far afield of those. Often her friend Pearl Schulman clipped a review from the New York papers and sent it to her, and Katie would then carefully forward it to me. My husband's relatives did the same for him, as "their writer." Family solidarity was being expressed, not readership—and between Katie and me that was enough. Enough to know that she approved of what I had done with my life.

Otherwise, I knew what I wanted of her. I wanted us to stay together, in the pristine time.

Now is she warning me that our wading time in the ever perfectible past is finally over? We have been like two long-haired girls hitching up our skirts in order to dip to the knee in what old verses used to call a laughing brook. Now are we to plunge into the present, in all our clothes?

We two can do that only through the past. That is our cousinship. What she wants of me now is to help her fill in the last corners of that concentric world we all leave behind us.

Where we might be now is at the rim of one of those ledged pools where, from whatever side you approach and descend into the central deep, the edges seem the same. Once you are in, up to the neck or even treading, the water's seal is perfect around you. Then, since you must, you can submerge. With grace.

As long as somebody knows it all?

"When you came out of the army . . . "

I see her in France in her uniform and army cap, under which hair bunned in the old-fashioned manner might add a feminine elegance beyond any of the then new curly bobs. There would have been men of all tastes over there, some of them veterans all too aware that in the well-run brothel, or behind those showcase windows where the prostitutes sit in Amsterdam or other knowledgeable cities, there is often a "military" type. The attraction of breasts behind sharp tailoring is a basic one—ask any office girl. Even we women ourselves feel it when so clothed, flattening our curves enticingly behind the buttons that hold, or flicking out sex at the point of a horsewoman's whip.

Add then the army, whose tailoring, on some missions not denied even to women, is always superb. And then, the idea behind "a nurse." To the coarse, any nurse is already partner to all the workings of the flesh. And that particular war was one in which even the rank and file could spell blond as *blonde*—hinkey dinkey parlez-vous.

On the other hand, there would have been all these romantic young marksmen from home—straight as flagpoles—whom war recruits for romance. For whom death would have been love's porn.

And to Katie? To that young nurse on the wards, clipped in her mock uniform, what would the wounded all around her be?

Not hypochondriacs.

"When you came out of the army, I recall the family saying you didn't look well."

How the aged manage to accumulate shadow around themselves—is it a talent of fading flesh? The room is actually no darker. Outside is the steady, almost boring Florida light, glaring with late-in-the-day optimism. We eat early here.

"Guess I didn't."

"Were you sick?"

"Guess I was."

"Like—dysentery, or something? Or one of those amoebic infections? That Americans only get when they go abroad?" I gave her a smile. Medical lingo always got her started.

A snort. "Nothing the awmy would increase my pension for."

Not for wounds they couldn't see. Yet Katie is proud of her military pension, received to this day. Is this why she feels no need to stand forth at the synagogue?

"Oh, I know they sent you with Mother because they trusted you." Did I? On tape, that sounded false.

Silence. The business with the compresses has stopped. There are silences like that between attendant nurse and patient, as I have been in hospitals enough myself to know. Late night sea silences with the bed becalmed, and patient telling nurse what the doctor doesn't know. When the illness is serious enough.

"Naw they didden!" She chokes on it. "Oh, maybe they trusted me to keep quiet on why she was going—but no more. When Clarence was dying I offered to look in on him for free; his bedsores were a sight. But Flora wouldn't give in."

Give in—*He wouldn't. . . . She won't. . . .* I hear the phrase the family used when we any of us were stuck in an attitude and nobody could find the scripture that would help us to get out.

"Tell you why they sent me." She's using that frail but stern midnight voice—the one that pauses only for truth. "Your mother trusted me. I was the only way they got her to go."

My mother could not bear to spend an hour in a house where there was an unpaid bill. She had the emigré's terrible need—and pride—not to owe. Some turn spend-thrift for the same reason. But not she. What had Katie given her that had broken down her German chill? What did she owe? I see the two of them in their corner, and their across-the-room glances.

"Because you had told her your troubles? In exchange for hers?"

Waiting for the patient, I listen to the humming of the refrigerator. We are in home care.

"I was young!" The voice is cracked.

And wounded? Where no one could see? Everyone saw my mother's wounds. But her main audience was against her.

"And desperate?"

I don't expect an answer. It's not something our cousin can admit. But misty as this room is, this dim semitropic for old bones, Katie of the brimming eyes is somewhere alive in it. So is cousinship. Cousins may kiss. Cousins may question. This has been my role, as cousin-child. Now the roles reverse. Now I am nurse as well.

When I was a kid I looked up the word *diphtheria* many times. All the dictionaries say the same thing. The membrane formed is tough. And what they call "false."

Many in my age group were among the first to be taught mouth-to-mouth resuscitation for the drowning. These days the rescue of the choking is by law a pinup in every city restaurant, though often hidden. The maneuver I perform requires the dark of family knowledge. I feel my mouth salivate with memory.

In the corner is that small, shrinking jaw, as ajar as a sick child's.

Bend deep, Hot-tense. Deeper than a kiss.

"They sent you down there to recover, too, didn't they, Katie? To the sea. I remember now."

I remember the waves at the windows. Constantly arriving, on a stretch of beach that seemed to me not far enough away for safety's sake. I knew that safety was somewhere involved. I remember the crashing of the sea in one's dreams, and the bunched sound of late-night crying when it is made by two people.

In the daytime the routine was morning pony rides for me and afternoon rides for all three of us in the rattan sedan-chairs that an attendant to each would wheel, my chair on the inside. Warmer there, and away from the conversation of the other two. But the wind mewling from under the boardwalk brings me their words, sifted with the blown sand under the pilings, and each day forgotten again, except for the name always centered in them, reappearing like a pebble does on the beach foam.

It was a slim Christian name, of the sort that would have slipped past one by the dozens in the good private schools of the time, eeling then into Wall Street—into banking more likely than into stocks—or else into one of the law firms whose names would be a string of its own kind. After which it would normally marry in a top church, acquire the appropriate affiliations and summer haunts—water being favored rather than mountains—and settle down to producing little candidates for good schools.

I didn't know any of this then. But even at seven I know the name as somehow different from ours, even from the Anglicized surnames like Clarence's, which was Winstock, or even my own. More important, I hear how when my mother pronounces it she does so with the same sugary lilt with which she alludes to certain New York families in "society," whose activities are reported in the newspapers, or whose members in one small way or another have touched her own circle—maybe met at a benefit performance at a Fifth Avenue townhouse, or sharing—before her marriage—the same modiste.

Vaguely I know that these people are all Christians, and of a special sort. My Aunt Jo—widow of my father's elder brother and middle-class Irish—was not included, nor were those male friends of my father's sporting days who still sometimes invited him to clubs like the New York Athletic Club, though he seldom accepted. Of certain other men whom I would hear of in my adolescence— judges and lawyers with names like Choate and Depew, whom he met at The Hundred Years Association, a club whose members either owned businesses or had other long-term connections with American commerce—I suspect she knew nothing. My father, who in Richmond had mingled with Christians since he was born, and whose sisters had gone to the convent, treated all this as ordinary. A Jew as proud as he could afford to condescend—and could not be condescended to. The only time I ever heard him guffaw at my mother was when she had suggested, if timidly, that we refer to ourselves as Hebrew, rather than

Jew. Later seeing him rub the permanently inflamed spots his pince-nez left to either side of the bridge of his nose—always a sign of his irritation, along with his almost inaudible "Harrumph."

And on that occasion I had heard one of my sardonic paternal aunts say to the other, not too under her breath, "Hattie wishes she had angels' blood."

So, rolling alongside sedately in my third chair, as the name, a man's, always said in full by Katie, came to rest with that certain relish on my mother's tongue—I at once took it to be the name of someone who must have had just such blood. Why else, when we were about halfway down the boardwalk and after some mournful interchange, would two people be weeping in unison and blowing their noses—except for one of those? I'd have been embarrassed in front of the attendants who wheeled us, except that from day to day the men who wheeled us were always new.

I am the attendant now. Katie's chair is stationary. Yet something is wheeling us both from behind; I hear its breath. Or is it Katie's, short and parched?

"Beck came to town to ask Daddy Joe. She hadn't been to the city in—not since I got my cap. My father had another woman there, Hot-tense. So Beck never went. Her life was in Port. And that's where I was—

"Yes?" Sometimes that's all a nurse has to say. But may have to repeat it. "Yes?"

"Lying . . . low." It came up like two bits of phlegm. "So Beck asked Father?"

See how I am saying Father, she Daddy Joe. We used to do that indiscriminately. He was father to so many. In the days when relationship was rightly one's role.

"She told him: 'My daughter's in mortal woe. So is your wife. Send them to cure together.' "

"And he arranged it."

"Never even asked her why." She is whispering now.

Yes, that would be his measure.

"Back at Port, Beck said to me: 'That man is worth his weight in gold, dollin'. But I didn't tell him your trouble. His women would have got it out of him.' "

Childhood's sensations are flooding me, mouth-to-mouth. I see my father as I used to see him, padding the corridors of his household like a peddler traversing his beat. One where the super-salesman of downtown is being sold something by somebody every hour of the day.

"So be it," he would say to me now. "Bend to your task, daughter. It is not necessary to know Hebrew."

"Your trouble. Want to tell me it, Katie?"

By one of those efforts that exceed the flesh, her face is reassembling, jaw closing evenly, fever gleam glossing the eyes. I see Katie when young. But not as I had ever seen her then. The hair an aureole, blown by the winds of France. The slim neck undamaged. The compress on her knees is a white cap—doffed.

She is as I would wish the women who were rifling my mother's bureau drawers to see her. No one is here to rifle her own memory-box except me.

"I always thought you a woman who would have been

loved by a man. That you must have had you—your love affair."

I hear only her breath, raucous with the past. Halfway across the room from her I can see the rise and fall of her old chest, and hear its soughing. But I have the power to see her as she was—and she knows it.

"There was a man's name. You and Mother used to bandy it between you. Riding by the ocean. It's on the edge of my—ear."

It mingles with the sea, and with all the surreal in any family. The letters dog-eared by one person's forefinger and thumb, and burned by another's. The names filtering on the wind outside the house, and not allowed in. The stories that no debtor can come to collect in exchange for cash.

"Down in Atlantic City you used to say the whole name, every time. Like Beck used to say 'Solly Pyle.' But not like it was the name of anybody that did you dirt."

That does it.

Is the sound she makes a chuckle, grounded way down—at me? Or the suck of a throat opening?

"Hon'—" I say. "Hon'."

The name comes up like a gout of freed air.

And that night the name, always said in full, first name and surname together, sometimes fluttered on her tongue like in a young girl's account of a date, sometimes marched through the bare facts like a theme worthy of two grown women crying over it in unison.

Why can't I remember it? Dick—Richard—Atwater? Or did Howard—or Howell—come in somewhere? The surname certainly had two syllables, maybe began with *H*. The first name sometimes shortened familiarly, but always with the second name following. I can hear the lilt. Or do I now compound it of beach voices and mild winter air just right for recovery? Plus what she told me as part of her plain but not meager sequel—that his family's money came from that first radio company of note, Atwater Kent?

In the few years left to her the name echoed once or twice between us; I could have repeated it to myself at any time. I never thought of writing it down. Now that she is dead, I find I have forgotten it, no matter how I try. Perhaps that is loyalty?

Or merely how the rescued child survives, yes, but only to tell imperfect tales?

I remember everything else.

"Beck knew," she's saying. "I couldn't trust a letter. But once during my service I came home on leave. And told her we were engaged."

"Nita know?"

"Naw." All her estimate of Nita is in that drawn-out syllable.

"Ayron?"

"You kidding?"

"But Mahma knew." Even now, she takes comfort from that. "He was a doctor, with the army. But not Jewish." She can smile now, when she says that. "He wanted me to go see his family, while I was on leave. So I went. One of those big townhouses, on Fifth."

"He wanted them to see *you*!"

She inclines her head, a little painfully, at my partisan-ship. "So he did, I guess. And they couldn't have been nicer."

"Southerners?"

"New England. But in New York a long time."

I see the house, see her there, that uniform, those eyes that offer their depth. How can they not approve their son's choice?

"They'd invited Beck to come, too, acourse, but she couldn't make herself—extend things that faw. I told them why. Solly Pyle would *never* . . . They couldn't have been—more understanding."

"So then what? Did Ayron find out?"

I could see him, the brotherly nemesis with the hook, throwing back the unwanted fish. Twice.

"Naw. Not that he could have done anything by then. Except create a fuss."

Not with the woman she had come to be—Katherine S. Pyle, as later her documents were always signed. I could see that now.

"Solly?"

Her head always lowered when she spoke of him. "I don't know what was hardest on Beck. That she couldn't tell him. Or that he wasn't there to tell." In the twist of her lip I see hard-soft old Beck saying that. "She said that after I went back overseas she spent more time on her knees than any Catholic."

"In synagogue?" I don't recall that we Jews spent much time on our knees there.

"Uh-uh. No—at home. She had to be careful not to show anything extra there. Sister and Brother thought it was because of Sol."

And her fiancé's family? Were they Catholics?

"Protestant. Congregationalists."

"Oh, those are some of the best," I hear myself say, encouraging her to marry, sixty years too late. "Daddy always said they were rather like the best of us." Rather like *us*, was what he had actually said. "Stern without orthodoxy. And just wishy-washy enough not to want to shed blood over it."

"Not over that," she said. "No."

"Then why didn't you?" I burst out. "You and he? Ever?"

The minute one says "ever," one knows why.

"He was keeled." She says it so quietly that for a minute the accent misleads me. I see a bright sail, keeling over and under. In gray weather.

He was killed shortly before the Armistice. Some doctors saw as much action as any officers, she said. Often without the same protections.

"He could have taken leave same time I did. But with what was going on out there, he couldn't bear to. He said, though, that I must do it for him. He wanted the family to know."

He was that kind, then. I was glad to know it. And sorry. And she was that kind. They could have made a life.

"I didn't break down until the Armistice. Then they had

to send me home. But a lot of us were being sent back normally. So no one but Beck knew the real reason for it."

"So you came down there, with Mother and me."

"And the sight of you cured me. Your mother mostly, of course. But you, too. Such an imp, you'd been. And turned so solemn, pore little puss."

"Our woes? Cured one like yours?"

She shook her head at me. "Uh-uh. I just remembered I was a nurse."

So, good-bye, doctor. Hathaway. Howard. I have recalled you. But there is no longer any need.

"Did you ever see them again? His family?"

"Oh, yes. His mother wanted to adopt me."

"Adopt you? A grown woman? What a— To be their— relic?"

"No, it wasn't like that. He was their only son. She wanted me to have his estate. 'If you'd had a chance to marry,' she said, 'you'd have had it. He'd want me to take care of you. And I want to.'"

She sat back. The coffee was cold but she sipped it. I saw the two of them, at tea.

"She was a lovely woman. And it was a fine house. Beautiful—but good, too. You know how it is, hon', when the people are good?" She lets that hang, a statement more than a question. Outside the ranch house, whose poreless, sheet-rock walls resist even ownership, that other household we had known together looms out of the night, an ark lifted on the hydrogen of memory—and sails on.

I don't answer her right away. In the style she and I were brought up in, we don't have to.

So it's she who resumes. We were chastised to respect the pace of the story even more than the revelation.

"But I could tell his mother wanted me for more than she knew. And so did he. A fine gentleman, a mite stiff. They dispensed their money, he said, as much as possible phil—what's the odd word?" She smiled, tired. "As charitably as they could."

"Philanthropically."

"That's it. And they said they thought I could do the same. They knew I'd interned at settlement houses."

"When people are good—" I said, reaching over to pat her.

"Oh, shoot—I could have fitted in there for right selfish reasons. It was the kind of house—well, I'd seen its like." She makes the sound I can no longer classify. "No shoats on Fifth Avenue, acourse. But I'd seen it all before. They wanted me for company, too. Would have wanted it, more and more. And I'd have had to deal with that." She sighs. "I knew places for that do-gooder money they wouldn't have got to on their own until kingdom come."

"Then why didn't you just go ahead and accept?"

"Because I couldn't do that to Beck."

"She'd have wanted you to."

"For sure. And for all the right reasons. So—I didn't tell her. She'd already asked me shouldn't she go there, under the circumstances, and pay her respects. 'That poor woman,' she said. But by then they were safely gone. To the Orient. She wrote a letter instead."

People of those days had a melodramatic way of keeping things from one another, grand-opera style. Letters that were somehow never sent—or arrived too late. Meetings that were forestalled; girls that were sent away—just in time. Was it that they wanted to blunt the edge of coincidence before it got to them? And call it fate?

"I'm not too fond of Patient Griseldas," I said.

Yet, maybe when your lover is killed just a few days before the Armistice, you crave even to counterpart on your own the vicious things that life can randomly do.

"You exaggerate easy," Katie says. "Y'always did."

I hear how even to reprove she uses the voice of the family. But how much honor must memory pay to self-sacrifice?

"What if you could have taken Beck with you?" I fling up my hands. "Sorry. One of the wild ideas that people on the sidelines give you gratis."

"Had it myself, thank you very much. She'd have fitted in like a glove. No one would have appreciated Beck more than them. But—"

"Nita."

"Nita?" The name conjures her, immovable as an inherited down pillow.

"I could have set Nita up separate. I thought of it. What Nita wanted more than anything was to make a place for herself in Port. She could've done a catering shop. She'd have bloomed. My first—philanthropy. I wouldn't have lived in the Fifth Avenue place—only nearby. Beck and I." I hear how even a lifetime later the dream can color the voice. "And after that—and I could have set it all up like a three-ring circus, don't think I couldn't—what a free nursing station and out-patient clinic Marnine Tooker and I could have run. Harlem Hospital isn't that far from upper Fifth Avenue."

She gets to her feet and stirs about in that musing movement which occurs in between the talk but is never pinpointed for the importance it has. Decisions flow then. Murder and fornication are contemplated. Sacrifices are clinched. Stirring about.

Katie, looking about her to ascribe it to something, seizes on the coffee tray, lifting it too smartly for her bent shoulders. I don't try to take it from her. It's the old black Tole tray, nearly a yard wide, that used to get sidetracked all over the Port house, whether freshly oiled and on end behind the wildflowers on the sideboard, or on the kitchen counter, steamy behind the jelly bag. She speaks to its center flowers. "Late in the day—for charitable words."

I hold my breath until she reaches the sideboard with that heavy thing. "Marnine Tooker. Wasn't that your friend from Atlanta, one you trained with?"

"Ah-huh. Heard from her until she died. Last year." She has her back to me. Waiting.

"Then, Katie—Katie—why didn't you do any of it?" That is a terrible thing to ask anyone. The tray, lifted like a weight, sustains her.

"Solly Pyle came home to die."

She clears the tray. It is returned to the sideboard. In Florida there is no place for it to wander much, no need.

And now, as sure as shinsplints—as we used to say, and whatever did that mean?—there she is hunting us an end-of-story drink.

The Victorian sideboard of that three-compartmented variety in which so many of the South kept their liquor predicts a certain bending to get to a bottle, and a clinking of the brass drawer handles above. I half close my eyes in order not to see—or to see—how Katie's shadow doubles and blurs into the many I have watched at this task at one time or another. I hear the blunt shove that even when heard from the next room always meant the closing of the sideboard's center door. The old word for a liquor supply was "requirements." One might hear the man of a house use it, in advance of a Sunday evening. "Have we the requirements?" was what was said.

Katie is bringing up the Kahlua—a full gift bottle, untouched—and a bottle of good brandy with a forlorn inch or two in it. "You had a friend—what was her name?—from Harlem."

I have to think a minute. "Arnella."

"The names they used to take—my. Those—Blacks." She sets out the newly furbished tray and turns to squint at me. She has to turn her whole body to do that now. "What happened to her?"

I haven't a clue. And Katie knows it.

"Okay, you win," I said. "We graduated. Into the North."

We each choose the brandy over the Kahlua, which sports a bright streamer citing its comparatively low alcohol content.

"Nothing that won't hurt you is that good for you," Katie says.

"Never heard that one."

"Old, old saw." She doesn't—as we used to say—expatiate.

I think: Sol's old saw.

She sees me think it.

In complete harmony, we drank.

We were eating nonpareils with the brandy when Clay rang—the all-round husband with the gift shelf.

He says he is fibrillating, a word much on the mind down here. Nothing for the ambulance, but for safety's sake would she come check him out?

"Not that kind of heart trouble old Clay is suffering from," she says, taking up the black satchel that hangs on the old "costumer" by the door. We say "hatrack" now—if we say it at all. "But I better go. Fact I'm bound to—that's our agreement."

I see she is proud of it. "Want company?"

"No, I'll drive. And I'm goin' give that lady-killer some homely *ad*vice."

In the doorway she stands, wan but gleeful, all the busted vertebrae aligning at duty's call. A single lady, but not unattended. What is safety?

"Remember that poster—the Red Cross Nurse?"

It was still in the grammar schools, long after the First World War. You would pay a premium for it now.

She nods, shrugs, grins—signaling some riposte already sweet on her tongue. "Why, honee child—" she drawls. "You still have on that fool hat."

I left a favorite pair of shoes down there. Over the phone afterward we laughed at that wishful implication and sometimes she would say, "You have to come pick up your shoes." We both knew I wouldn't come again. She because she was wise in the way of families, whose members at the crucial moment will often spare themselves pain—even because they do love.

I told myself something even harsher: that the habit of the recorder, once a life is recognized as perfectly rounded, is to bow out.

At times during the next year I would hear of her genealogical tussles with a researcher who had misspelled Boettigheimer or incorrectly placed her grandfather, Daniel Hart Pyle; once I sent her notice of a Dutch reference book, eighteenth century, edited by a Pyle, that I had come across at the Newberry Library. Now and then she repeated her resentments at Aaron's family—the old debt, the silence of the niece at whose marriage she and Nita had ceded those early family artifacts. And once she sent me some fragments of stories that Nita had written—one in particular on an encounter they had both witnessed when young, between Solly's other woman and Beck, who had routed her from the house.

But in the main we spoke of her telephone friends, as if they were also mine. Of Dr. Siletsky in "Gret Nick," who was "like a son" to her. I sensed she was looking forward to her will, where both justice and affection would be meted out. And also felt a satisfaction that her resources, whatever they were, would be enough for such display. She did not ask me again whether I was "all right."

Death came on via a stroke not as quick as she would have wished, at the veteran's hospital elsewhere in Florida, to which she had afterward been removed on her own instructions in event of such. A nurse friend, detailed to be in charge, and over the phone during Katie's last days a little proprietary for being in at the death as I was not, informed me: "No point in coming down. No telling what she understands. She can't talk."

I thought of her in bed—choked. And knowing. I thought of myself on such a bed—as one does.

She died.

The small chest of drawers arrived, listed by the appraisers as Viennese, and perhaps it was, stepping out of its multifold wrappings on thin, cabriole legs. With it came a delicate French watch on a chain, its origin not given, and Beck's broad wedding band, initialed S.A.P. to R.B., September 15th, 1891. I felt that sense of kinship, burden, and submission which such objects always gave me. All objects cling to us under threat to dominate our days. I will help them to live, knowing full well that they may outlive me, but under warning that at any minute I may throw them over. I believe that all of us, from the pack rats that most of us are to the true collector, are in the end filled with this delicious vengeance. We are trying to penetrate the mystery of the inanimate, and to take arms against the material presence by owning it. All the while knowing that its tidal wave will pass over us, and on.

Within that unanimous inanimate which one cannot ever really warm into syllable, the inherited object has a viciously tender advantage, and the domestic ones are the worst. A diamond is easy, or a camelback sofa; shut away in a safe, sell. Or find another relative. But what is one to do with one's mother's poultry shears, that nine out of ten are better than one could buy today? Keep them, and listen to the sputter of the fricassee.

A will is such an object. It almost always finds its mark—as Katie's did. Even the freight charge for the little chest had been taken care of, as were all possible costs for us "good" legatees, while a firmly opposite clause hedged off her small company of villains by reason of their indebtedness, and cast them out. It was plain that Katie had tidied and retidied her affairs not only so that all left behind her received their just deserts, but so that the receding landscape of her life could be seen for the last time, stringently clear. I thought of a head nurse's desk, as I had sometimes seen such a corner when convalescent in hospital and walking down the hall—the glowing lamp, the pencil by the pad, all patients' record sheets handy and all emergency systems blinking—only the nurse herself not there.

After a will, there is a certain convalescence, too. During that period Katie's actual cousin Charles, whose name I had met for the first time in that document, wrote to me. A retired civil servant living in Baltimore, he had inherited the Port Charlotte house, which he and his family would use winters, after it was brought up from what he indicated was a bad state of repair. The letter was amply courteous in that exactly mid-Southern style which I have always allotted to the Marylanders. Not as crusty-uppity as we Virginians can be—as if we are suddenly chewing rose hips along with our bent diphthongs. Nor yet as glottally laid back as Georgia or Tennessee. The gentle responsibility that wafts from the letter is healing; though strangers, we have shared an intimate death.

But it is the mannerliness that most rushes me back. Clarence, or any of the men of my father's circle, could have written such a letter, or even perhaps that poor collage of a man—barber-pole body, toothbrush moustache, and cigarette in two fingers—the untrustworthy bookkeeper. Who, I only now recall, was as nice to me as if he were not a known miscreant, only rather furtively, as if his good qualities, too, were about to be found out. I see the poker table, at which he—I realize now—must not have been allowed to play. Bent at the waist as if still hunched over his doubtful books, dangling his fag in contrast to the players' Garcia Vegas, present in our family bosom only because of his sister, our sister-in-law Belle, now herself a renegade, he watches hungrily—inscribed in a child's brain and waiting to tell her his last name: Leeman, Harry B.

But what Charles has to tell me about Katie is the real shocker. Had I ever heard that Katie herself wrote stories? She once told him she had, publishing them under an assumed name. But would never tell him more, except that the income from them had been given to charity. He wished now to enlist my help in finding them in order to set all to rights and pay her memory its proper due.

The shock to me was not so much that she had written. Everyone has memory, fantasy, and a will to record; a handful of us turn professional. Once you are so, you become aware that all the world's readers are in some sense what you are. Only a lack of your excessive need to exercise that sensibility, or of "talent" as some have the sad grace to say, has kept them amateur. I can never answer them— even the ones who say: "I'd write, but I have to give my time to more important things"—except with a full and grateful throat at my own happenstance, or else a private laugh. I used to tell students that for the many who have the linguistic equipment to be a writer—a serious one— the rest is stamina, and some luck. During my middle years I would have added: and character, not necessarily all good, but there. Now I would add: a willingness to be burdened by the overview—plus an inability to escape it.

Were the few pages shown me as Nita's by Katie, and still somewhere in my archives, really Katie's? I think not; she would not have been that deceptive. They were given me as family record. Yet don't I seem to recall that at one time she did say, really only mention, that she had once written some stories herself, even publishing some? I must have said I'd like to see them; I would surely have said that. But she made so little of it—I think I remember—that I must have backed off, especially so if she told me the money went to charity. There are quasi-publications that do this; perhaps her stories were anecdotes of her nursing life? Or perhaps they were not. The shock is that in my mind I assigned them there, or to some other quasi-place. I listened with the hauteur of the professional.

Do I have regrets over the possible stories themselves? Not much more than for curiosity's sake. I think Katie herself only wanted us to know—so much. Family knowledge among us was many-layered; much or maybe all was known, but not all was talked about. That, too, contributed to the sense of clan. Briefly I did regret that I hadn't paid more honor to the fact that she, too, was a recorder—on the page. Then I saw what she must have, that for me to become in any way the mentor or the authority would not have done, was not in her idea of us. Rather, our twosome must preserve what by reason of regional and family habit and my side's eccentric generational mixups we so happily were—two ponderers, one always up ahead, one just precocious enough to keep in step.

One step more. Do I feel I have here in these pages exposed what she might have kept secret? Not at all. If she was trained by her era not to expose, it was ambivalently, for at the same time there was all that family leeway of ours, by which the covert gossip as to what did happen could go merrily, dramatically on. What Katie has done, before death and even after, is to preempt me to her service, just as she preempted my mother's. She always had the strictest sense of what was owed, by her and to her. She still instructs me as to how love can pay. She was my nurse.

So, this Sunday afternoon I have just telephoned Charles, I am not quite sure why. To be sure of my facts? To let him know I am writing this? Or because the solo flight of the mnemoniac is performed in an Arctic chill extreme?

Charles is the grandson of Aunt Beck's sister. In our long, random conversation he tells me she was entirely lacking in Beck's humor. As for the stories: "Katie got involved with a group of young people who were doing such things. The money she received went to an orphanage." He is disappointed to hear that Aaron's wife, Leona, to whom I had written at his suggestion, knew nothing of this, although he is interested to hear that she answered me—as she would not have answered him. I scent the acrid, burnt-out smell of old feuding—that air was stimulating once. Feuding families are usually strong families; the warring is in part how they keep themselves vibrant in the world; let the world hear their drum and brassy twang.

Charles, who does not lack humor, wants to talk about Nita, whom I surmise he liked more than I.

Did I know she was a graduate chemist—City College—and that she once was Eddie Cantor's secretary? Quit, because he wouldn't give her the Jewish holidays—

wouldn't believe she was a Jew. "Made a fuss about giving his own Social Security back to the government—but wouldn't give his secretary that."

A lovely anecdote, but at first hard to reconcile with the Nita I knew—her plump fastness of breasts neatly held in, but down whose crack a crumb now and then disappeared. So she quit, did she?—not much else a woman could maybe do, then. But the harder she quit, the harder Katie coped.

I take another tack to ask about Katie's fiancé. Yes—"he was killed in the war." Charles does not recall his name, but his wife might; I hear him call out to her: "Jeanette!" No, at the moment she can't summon it.

So, that young doctor who stayed with the wounded, and now himself a skull, is scrabbled for maybe the last time—by two strangers to him and to each other, on the phone from New York to Baltimore. I think of how an individual life winds down to less and less mention—toward the last. These are the mnemoniac scraps. Our world rains with them, invisible but everywhere. I myself cannot linger much longer here—even for Katie Pyle.

And was it all preamble, this? In the course of writing this, I have sometimes stopped myself, saying: It's all preamble; when does the story begin? The answer is in the verb: it began. And daily begins. Memory is the marching companion of the consciousness; it pulses in our fingertips as we live and breathe and cram our mouths and twist in the sexual bed—and fade. That's why some people believe in heaven. Surely this preamble life, so vigorous, so organized even to its goose-step wars, or so wandering the fields of family voice, must point, surely points somewhere? To the final burst of bloom that is the simple soul's Eden come round again? To the honey-ooze of all our molecules into—a status quo? *Uh*-uh. No Sunday School certifies a heaven for the Jews. We believe in a Messiah. That gets us off the hook.

So, Katie, let us sum up. For it is us, isn't it? There were two cousins here all along. The younger cousin had her elder cousin keep on later in the day than a child born to that crowd—even if to a younger mother—could have hoped. Having such an elder stretches the time span. The elder cousin had a quondam daughter, almost. Each of them without obligation. Yet there are people who cannot die until we do. I have a host of those now. You may not be the last. Wearing Beck's broad wedding band, as I often do, brings that vivid host before me, most of them as unknown to her as she to them. Wearing it tells me who I am.

Katie, I hear the word "give" in all its uses. Give; give in; never give up. I see us prying for safety in all the corners behind our army of chairs. And what was safety, for us? A place in which you played for time in which to weave stories. How can we hold anyone safe in our arms except there?

What are family stories except exorcism? Answer: celebration. We celebrate the future of what was. So it is best to dedicate this story to a relative, preferably young, and of the blood. In this case a Katy of a different spelling, a girl with brown teacup eyes.

"You don't sound Southern at all," she said once, hearing some of our history.

I could have answered her the way I do in England, where I am said not to sound American: Oh, I'm a parrot. I talk like whoever's on the bus. Or I could turn granny coy and say: I've a tape in my head that pulls me this way, that.

What I want most to do is to expatiate, prevaricate, take her on my knee and squeeze her to me and back into her own history, while I enunciate a list of words that are strange ones to make the eyes brim: *kibosh, costumer, davenport*. But it is hard to weasel out when facing one's own eyes in duplicate. So I widen mine—which action seems to hold back departed words quite satisfactorily. "I only spoke Southern for a time."

Long or short—that expresses it. Katie is dead now. And I am from the North.

Have I caught all the fish then, Katie—and tossed them back?

Katie—are you all right?

FINIS

About the Author

HORTENSE CALISHER is the author of numerous works of fiction and an autobiography, *Herself*. A former president of P.E.N., she is the president of the American Academy of Arts and Letters. She lives in Manhattan and upstate New York.